Kingston Libraries

The Raven's
CHILDREN

YULIA YAKOVLEVA

Translated from Russian by Ruth Ahmedzai Kemp

PUFFIN

PUFFIN BOOKS

UK | USA | Canada | Ireland | Australia
India | New Zealand | South Africa

Puffin Books is part of the Penguin Random House group of companies
whose addresses can be found at global.penguinrandomhouse.com.

www.penguin.co.uk
www.puffin.co.uk
www.ladybird.co.uk

First published in the English language by Puffin Books 2018

001

Translated from Russian by Ruth Ahmedzai Kemp
Original text copyright © Yulia Yakovleva, 2016
English-language translation copyright © Ruth
Ahmedzai Kemp, 2018
Cover illustration copyright © Lauren O'Hara, 2018

Set in 11.5/15.5 pt Bembo Book MT Std by Jouve (UK), Milton Keynes
Printed and bound in Great Britain by Clays Ltd, Elcograf S.p.A.

A CIP catalogue record for this book is available from the British Library

ISBN: 978-0-241-33077-7

All correspondence to:
Puffin Books
Penguin Random House Children's
80 Strand, London WC2R 0RL

For Boris, my grandfather,
and his sisters Katya, Tamara and Lida

CHAPTER ONE

Shura saw Valya waving to him from further along the track. The air was full of railway smells: smoke and coal. Grey clouds hung low over the city, and even they looked like puffs of steam out of an engine's funnel. The huts and sheds were silhouettes against the low sun. The signal flashed. From time to time, a whistle or a horn ripped through the air, or metal clanked as carriages were coupled.

The ground was stripy with rails packed close together. Sleepers, splattered with oil, ran off into the distance like black piano keys. Trains rumbled past, slowing down as they approached the platform and gradually picking up speed as they chugged away.

Leningrad was a beautiful city, but it was the railway yard that Shura loved best of all – this hidden part that passengers didn't see. Here the crammed-close tracks ran in parallel streams like a river of metal. Later they went their separate ways, somewhere in the distance, further away than Shura could see. Onward they ran over the horizon, each following its own path over the vast expanse of the Soviet Union. Onward to Moscow, Kiev, Stalingrad, Molotov, Tashkent, Kirov, Vladivostok, the Urals, Siberia, towards mountains, seas and oceans. Whenever Shura stood on the rails, he could feel the gentle buzz running through them like they were nerves, and through the soles of his feet he could sense the hum of life in far-flung towns.

He never told Valya about it, even though he was his best friend. Valya would have laughed at him – he was no-nonsense, practical. He had five younger brothers and sisters, and together with their mother, they all squeezed into one room in a communal flat on Marata Street. Valya had no time for idle daydreaming.

Shura carefully arranged the objects along the rail: a nail, a copper coin, a nut and another nail. He looked up.

'You asleep or what?' Valya called as he came closer. 'I was shouting and waving. Didn't you see me?' He rested his foot, in its filthy, scuffed boot, on the rail. 'Not like that,' he tutted, inspecting Shura's work with a self-important air. He spread the objects further apart. 'Otherwise they'll all squash together into one pancake.'

Valya laid out his own collection on the other rail of the same track: a few nuts and bolts, a small tin bullet, some nails. The boys hopped over the rails to the embankment, running through the slushy March snow into the bushes, where they waited, chatting to fill the time until the next train came along to turn their offerings into warm, satisfyingly thin metal wafers.

'*Shhh*,' Valya whispered.

From time to time, the stationmaster would make his rounds of the tracks. In his sheepskin coat and overalls that were smeared with grease, he would poke around here and there with his iron crowbar, then continue on his way.

But it wasn't him this time; it was a policeman in a greatcoat with a dog.

'Alsatian,' said Valya. 'A sniffer dog.'

They crept deeper into the bushes and froze. Shura saw one of his footprints fill with grey water. The bushes were bare and gave little cover.

But either the dog wasn't expecting to stumble upon two boys in the railway yard, or perhaps it just wasn't in the mood to waste time with something so frivolous. It clearly had more important business. The dog tugged on its lead, occasionally wagging its bushy tail in impatience.

'I wonder who they're looking for.'

'A pickpocket, maybe?'

'Who knows,' said Valya, in a weighty tone. 'Perhaps it's on high alert, ready to catch spies. Or they're tracking enemies of the state . . . to stop them derailing a train.'

They watched in silence.

There was a whistle, a clatter. The signal changed from red to green. The moist air began to fill with the heavy rumble of an approaching train.

'A freight train,' Valya predicted.

Both would have preferred a passenger train. The cheerful steamers with all their little windows were much lighter and didn't flatten the metal objects quite so thin. You ended up with a squashed version of the object, so a nail would leave the outline of a mushroom and a nut would leave a faint hexagon.

Puffing and panting, a dark-green steam engine chuntered past, slowly-slowly. It was pulling a train of brown wooden wagons with padlocks on the doors and no windows, but there were gaps between the wooden boards – presumably to let the air in.

'Oh!' Shura gasped, just stopping himself from shouting. 'Did you see that?'

'See what?'

'Eyes – looking out through one of the cracks!'

'So? Could be cows. Or horses.' But Valya's voice didn't sound very confident.

Another wagon. More cracks. More eyes.

'Hey! Did you see?'

'All right, shut up. Yes, I saw.'

They both felt uneasy. Those were definitely people's eyes. People staring out.

Another wagon. More eyes. Another wagon. Yet more eyes. Wagon. Eyes. Wagon. Eyes. Its wheels rattling, the train kept on going, pulling these huge wooden wagons. It was a train longer than anything Shura had ever seen. And there were eyes. Eyes. Eyes. Eyes.

Suddenly something shot out from one of the wagons. Something white, the size of a marble, bounced off the embankment and rolled across the snow. It fell into a soggy puddle in a footprint in the snow.

Valya made a dash for it.

'Where are you going?' hissed Shura.

Valya deftly grabbed the tiny ball, then dived back into their hiding place.

'Show me!' said Shura, pushing to see.

'It's mine,' Valya warned. 'I found it!'

'Fine! But let me see!'

As the train rumbled by, they smoothed out what turned out to be a ball of crumpled-up paper. It had some writing on it. The purple ink was slightly smudged in the patches where the paper had got wet.

'Well?' asked Valya impatiently.

'Er, that's an "a". And that's a "vuh". Um, that's "muh".'

'Muh-muh-muh! I thought you could read.'

'I'm only in class one!' Shura protested. He was just seven and wasn't reading very long words yet.

Valya nudged his shoulder and pointed. As the final wagon of the train passed by, its tail lamps – two red eyes – stared at them as though bidding farewell. Valya shoved the scrap of paper inside his flat cap and pulled it down tight on his head.

They hopped out from the bushes and ran over to the rails to inspect their spoils. The wet snow squelched under their boots.

'Dammit,' said Valya, disappointed.

Shura scraped his fingernail along the rail. It was still hot from the passing train's wheels. Their treasure was completely flattened, firmly welded into the metal. Their objects had become splodges of different colours on the rails: a splash of copper, tin, lead.

'Well, it was a long one, that's for sure,' commented Shura.

'I've never seen one as long as that.'

'Who do you think those people were?'

'Passengers.'

'Didn't look like a passenger train.'

'Soldiers, perhaps. On a secret mission. That's why they could only peer through the cracks like that.'

Shura remembered the huge padlocks on the wagon doors. 'Maybe thieves?'

'There aren't that many in the Soviet Union,' said Valya. 'It's not like America.'

'How do you know?'

'It says so in the papers.'

Shura felt annoyed by his know-it-all friend. 'You can't even read!'

'Shame about my coin,' said Valya, changing the subject. 'We could have bought some fizzy drinks with it.'

But he didn't sound very upset about it. After all, it wasn't like him to be grumpy.

Shura and Valya slipped in the damp slush, and jumped off banks of heaped-up snow and junk lying on the ground, as they cut through the yards and back lanes towards the River Ligovka.

They were back in the city now. The straightness of the broad avenue was emphasized by the tall houses, tightly packed together, grey and dilapidated with age, their paint chipped and peeling.

It was trying to snow, but not really managing to; it was a drizzly sleet that sprinkled down on the passers-by. All in a rush, they scurried this way and that against the musical background of tram bells ringing and the occasional car impatiently tooting its horn.

The boys turned into a side street. The mucky, slushy snow came up to their knees and the buildings here were damp and dripping.

Valya's home, on Marata Street, was a stone's throw from

here. But Shura's was another five blocks away, past the market, on Pravda Street.

It was time for them to go their separate ways. Shura would get an earful if he was seen with Valya, who he wasn't allowed to play with. Shura's parents were at work, but if his neighbours spotted him with Valya they'd dob him in.

An idea came to Shura, out of the blue. 'What if I give you a nail for it?' he suggested.

'What?' said Valya. He obviously didn't realize what Shura was talking about it.

Shura couldn't take his mind off the scrap of paper they'd found. Who had thrown it out of the train? Why? Who was it for?

'What? The bit of paper?' said Valya.

'Maybe it's a map?' said Shura. 'Buried treasure?'

'You wish! It's just a piece of paper.' But Shura could tell from Valya's expression that he was starting to think otherwise.

'Chuck it away, then, if it's just a piece of paper.'

They crossed Marata Street. But Valya hadn't noticed where they were.

'Swap it for a cartridge?' offered Shura. A bullet cartridge was something very valuable. Valya hesitated.

Shura didn't need the piece of paper; he was just curious. He was always nosy and interested in everything, always eager to find out about things and try things out.

Valya didn't need it either. Shura knew it. But when he saw how Shura's eyes were twinkling with curiosity, he immediately changed his mind. If the piece of paper was worth a cartridge, then he definitely wanted it for himself.

'Leave it. It's mine.'

'Are you my friend or what?' Shura wasn't going to give up easily.

'I found it.'

'We both found it at the same time!'

'You just sat there in the bushes!'

The sandy-coloured market hall stretched along beside them. It was a short, fat sort of building with peeling paint. Women scurried about under the covered walkway carrying baskets with milk bottles peeking out of the top. Shura and Valya passed a cart where a man wearing mittens was unloading boxes.

'We were both hiding!' Shura protested.

'I picked it up!'

'But I would have picked it up too!'

'Why didn't you, then? Scaredy-cat.'

Shura was affronted. 'You think I'm a scaredy-cat?' Annoyed, he gave Valya a little shove. Just gently.

Valya wobbled on the slippery ground, but steadied himself. He shoved Shura back, then gave him another push for good measure. Valya ran off. Shura chased after him.

Suddenly Shura realized they were by his home. Seeing this was his last chance, Shura caught up with Valya and swiped at his cap, which flew off, sending the piece of paper along with it. While Valya snatched at his cap, Shura let out a triumphant shriek as he grabbed the paper.

'Give it back, you rat! I found it!' Valya yelled, jumping about, trying to snatch it from Shura. Not a chance.

'I'm not giving it back!'

'It's like that, is it?' said Valya, as he let go of Shura. 'Then I'm not your friend any more!'

'Good riddance!' yelled Shura, pushing him away.

Valya spat at him. 'Don't even think about coming with me to see Papanin tomorrow!'

The whole city was buzzing with preparations to welcome home the Soviet heroes Ivan Papanin and his team of polar explorers, and Shura was as excited as anyone else at their return. The explorers had spent weeks adrift on a melting ice floe, their lives in grave danger. The whole country had been tirelessly following events on the radio and scouring the newspapers for the latest news of their icy captivity. Eventually Soviet ice-breakers and aeroplanes had come to the rescue, and the great heroes were due to arrive in Leningrad tomorrow. Shura couldn't wait to see the ceremonial parade through the city, when they would be driven from the port in open-topped cars with flags, with an orchestra playing and a motorcycle escort.

For a second, Shura wanted to throw the stupid scrap of paper on to the pavement. But instead he shouted back, 'As if I need to go with you! I'll go by myself!'

Valya shook his fist at him, already a few paces away. 'Just wait. Come anywhere near me tomorrow and I'll skin you alive!'

'Ooh, I'm really scared,' Shura teased. He stuck his tongue out.

At that, Valya grabbed a piece of brick from a broken stretch of wall, took a swing and hurled it at Shura.

SMASH!

*

'You'll pay me now for the glass!'

Several hours later Shura's father and their neighbour Auntie Dusya stood facing each other like boxers in a ring. She lived downstairs from Shura, in a communal flat on the ground floor of their building. He'd never been in her room before. Auntie Dusya was a large woman, with big red hands. Her room, by contrast, seemed small, poky and dark with soot. It was even darker now that a piece of cardboard covered the window in place of the broken pane.

'Shura, who broke the window?' asked Papa.

'It's obvious who it was!' shrieked Auntie Dusya. 'That delinquent!'

Papa frowned. 'Wait. So it wasn't my son? Who, then?'

'It wasn't my fault,' mumbled Shura.

'Oh yes, it was your fault. It most definitely was!' Auntie Dusya shook her fist in the air, as though she imagined she could summon a new windowpane out of thin air if she waved her hand hard enough. 'You brought him here, that delinquent! That hooligan! And you just stand there with your hands in your pockets like it's nothing to do with you!'

'Valya isn't a *dedink . . . ledink . . .*'

'Shura, stop clowning around,' said Papa. 'And take your hands out of your pockets.'

Shura sighed and pulled his hands out of his pockets.

'Have you been playing with that Valya again?' Papa's forehead crumpled into a frown. 'Answer me, Shura.'

Shura took a deep breath.

'He was!' Auntie Dusya squealed. 'He was with him again! I saw them with my own eyes. I'll never get a kopeck from that delinquent! They're beggars, the lot of them! His mother works at the factory, kids coming out of her ears! He's always roaming the streets, getting up to mischief . . . breaking people's windows!'

'He wasn't aiming at the window!' Shura insisted in Valya's defence. 'He was aiming at *me*!'

Auntie Dusya rolled her eyes and sighed.

'Listen, there's no need to shout,' Papa said calmly.

That was the last straw: Auntie Dusya turned crimson with rage.

Papa pulled his wallet out of his pocket. 'OK, what do we owe you for the window?'

'No ice cream for you this month,' warned Papa when they had walked upstairs to their flat and shut the door of their room behind them. 'And I'm afraid there'll be no cinema for you either, for a whole month. To think you'd cross that woman, of all people! Could you not choose a friendlier neighbour if you're going to break someone's window?'

'Ilya!' Mama scowled at Papa.

'Be thankful she didn't eat us alive,' Papa said to Shura.

Shura made to say something.

'I don't want to hear it, Shura,' Mama said. 'That's enough from you.'

Mama had been ironing and was now putting the laundry in the wardrobe. Shura's little brother, Bobka, was trying to help, which meant he was getting in the way. He was only three, so he was always getting in the way.

'So, glass is expensive these days, it turns out,' Papa remarked to Mama. 'Can you believe it –?' He suddenly stopped and bent down. 'What's this?'

Shura froze. He felt in his pocket – the paper was gone!

Father was holding it, reading it to himself. He squeezed his lips together so they all but disappeared. Anxiously he glanced at the door, then at Mama. She came over and read it, too.

'*Tell them . . . 5 Sadovaya Street . . . taken to Kolyma Gulag . . .* Who's this from?'

Both parents stared at Shura.

'Answer us, Shura,' insisted Mama, her face white. 'Who gave this to you?'

'Nobody.'

'Don't you dare lie! Tell me the truth!'

Bobka's face quivered when Mama shouted; he was on the verge of tears. Mama picked him up.

'Look what you've done!' she shouted at Shura.

'I'm not lying! I found it!'

'Where did you find it?' asked Papa. His voice was serious. 'Where?'

Shura didn't speak. He was strictly forbidden to go to the railway station, let alone anywhere near the tracks. Let alone with Valya!

'Oh, this boy will be the death of me,' muttered Mama, collapsing on to a chair.

'Shura, listen to me. A bad person wrote this,' explained Papa. 'A criminal who's been punished by our Soviet nation.'

Shura felt as if his heart was being crushed. Papa always knew how to make Shura feel guilty.

12

'Who have you shown it to? Has Tanya seen it?'

Shura shook his head. Tanya, his big sister, wasn't home yet. She went to school in the afternoon and she was always back late.

'Tanya's still at school,' Mama confirmed. Her face was very pale.

'So,' said Papa. 'I hope you're not lying. I'm going to throw this away. As if it never existed. Do you understand? And not a word about it outside these walls. Understand?'

Shura nodded, biting his lip.

'Or it could have disastrous consequences.'

Shura burst into tears. Bobka, who was sitting on Mama's lap, saw him and immediately started crying, too.

'I'm telling you – he'll drive me to an early grave!' Mama exclaimed.

'Shura,' Papa said, trying to make his voice sound calm, 'I'm not angry. You didn't know. But this . . . this bad person – this criminal – left this note on purpose, to get whoever finds it into trouble. Do you understand?'

Shura nodded. He wiped his tears with the palm of his hand. 'Is that why they were in big wagons with padlocks on?'

'What wagons?' Then Mama realized. 'Were you playing on the tracks again?'

Shura started sobbing. His shoulders began to shake.

'Shura,' Papa said, stroking his head. 'There's no place in Leningrad for criminals like that among honest, good people. That's why they were taken away in locked wagons. Do you understand? But that's beside the point. We're not telling you off for going to the station.'

'Excuse me,' Mama objected. 'We most certainly are!'

'If anyone hears about this, it'll be very hard to prove that you found this note by accident,' Papa continued in a serious voice. 'You understand? Not a word about this to anyone.'

Shura nodded, still sobbing. Papa gave him a hug. He stroked his back. Then he walked over to the table and found a cigarette lighter in a drawer. He snapped it alight and set fire to the paper and threw it into the ashtray to burn.

'Now there's nothing to worry about,' he said, his voice cheerful again.

They watched the paper curl up at the sides as the flame consumed it.

The door clicked. Papa flinched and Mama leapt to her feet.

It was Tanya, home from school.

'Oh, you made us jump,' said Mama.

Tanya dropped her satchel to the floor.

'What's that smell of burning?'

'It's —' Shura started.

'Your father's been burning some old papers,' Mama hurriedly explained.

'Ah,' replied Tanya, not really interested. Then she suddenly livened up, as though she'd tuned the radio to something more interesting. 'Guess what happened at school today! At break-time. I was sitting with the girls on the windowsill and —'

'Shura,' Papa interrupted, 'we haven't finished. The railway station — that's another matter entirely. You're not playing outside for a month. Especially not with Valya. And you're not going to Nevsky to see Papanin tomorrow. To school and then straight home for lunch! Do you hear me?'

'Is he in trouble?' Tanya's face lit up. 'What did he do?'

Shura pulled a face at her.

'Tanya, sit down and eat,' Mama said. 'But first wash your hands!'

'Shura, did you understand what I said?' his father asked, in a quiet but weighty voice.

'Yes, Papa,' Shura murmured.

Tanya carried on chattering away. 'So, what's he been up to this time? Hanging around with that mate of his again? I knew it! Anyway, you'll never guess what happened today. We were sitting . . .'

CHAPTER TWO

Shura dashed out of the door on to the street. The door slammed behind him. Auntie Dusya's window seemed to glare at him reproachfully with its cardboard eye-patch, as if threatening to report him to Papa. But the whole matter about being grounded . . . that was yesterday and Shura was too excited about what today had in store to worry about his parents finding out.

The day was smiling and it smelt of spring.

Shura ran and ran – through the streets, over the bridge across the River Fontanka – all the way to Nevsky Prospekt, Leningrad's main boulevard. That was where Papanin and his expedition team would be driving past in their convoy.

The whole city was buzzing with excitement about the heroes' arrival. The houses seemed to be standing to attention, tall and straight, with their decorative plasterwork like soldiers' medals and epaulettes. The rhythmic drip-drip of melting snow was like the March sunshine tapping its finger on the windowsills and porch roofs.

Golden smiles of sunlight flickered on the walls of buildings and glints of light sparkled on Leningrad's countless streams and canals, usually a dull, murky yellow-grey. Slushy

16

snow had been scraped to the edges of the pavement, and even in these grey mountain ranges of heaped-up, thawing ice the sunshine glimmered on individual crystals, sparkling like minuscule diamonds. Even the seagulls flying over the wide River Neva looked like they'd had a good scrub for the occasion – they were gleaming white like starched napkins with stiff corners.

Shura hurtled down the street, his feet barely touching the ground. Splashes went flying as he tore through puddles, but nobody minded. Nobody hissed like they usually did when he rushed past – they were all smiles today. Everyone knew today was special. Everyone knew where all the girls and boys were running to.

Shura sprinted past the ballet school, where the white columns across the front stood tall and proud like a row of ballerinas.

'Watch it!' said a woman with a string shopping bag, who only just managed to jump out of his way.

Shura dashed round the corner, skirting the huge yellow theatre with Apollo up there on the roof, driving his horse-drawn chariot in his short-skirted toga. Apollo had the best view in town, Shura realized, a little envious.

In the public gardens at the front of the theatre, the black silhouettes of bare trees shivered; Shura thought that their poor toes must be frozen from standing in damp snow. Or perhaps it was the wind that made them tremble. The cast-iron statue of Empress Ekaterina, set high on her enormous platform, was craning her neck, as though she were also impatient to catch a glimpse of the famous polar explorers.

Both sides of the broad avenue of Nevsky Prospekt were crammed with noisy crowds. Occasionally someone would dash across the road, and the policemen in their helmets would let out a shrill cacophony of whistles. Their warnings didn't scare anyone but just added to the cheerful, restless mood.

Shura plunged himself merrily into the crowd, pushing his way through with his elbows.

Everyone was standing very close together, like on the trams in the morning rush-hour. On the tram, though, people were normally sleepy and grumpy, but today everyone seemed perfectly content about being squashed up so tightly, as though this infectious good cheer were hopping from person to person. It seemed like the snow was thawing today from the happy warmth these people were radiating. Even the soggy black crows weren't screeching their usual *crah, crah*; today their call sounded more like *hurrah! hurrah!*

'They're coming! They're coming!' the crowd chanted, as the excitement surged along Nevsky Prospekt. Shura could hear the marching band approaching – a rumble in the distance.

Shura laughed along with everyone else around him. It was a shame Valya wasn't here – it would have been even more fun with his friend. But what could he do? They'd make friends again somehow.

'Look up there!' someone shouted.

Shura looked up. Three aeroplanes with bright-red stars on their wings were flying very low along the course of Nevsky Prospekt, showing their grey bellies. A swarm of white pieces of paper flowed out behind them like a tail – messages welcoming the heroes home. People were jumping about and grabbing them as they fell.

Shura leapt and waved his hands about, trying to grab one, too, but he kept missing.

Then – yes! He got one! He snatched it right in front of a lady's nose.

He tucked it inside the top of his coat. It'd be good to get one for Valya, too. And one for his sister, Tanya. And for little Bobka. And maybe two more, for Mama and Papa.

'Hurrah!' Shura shouted, beside himself with joy. 'Hurrah!'

Carried away by his excitement, Shura snatched at another flyer, not realizing that someone else had already grabbed the other end. Shura looked up to see a tall boy in a cap glaring at him.

'Let go, you little runt,' he snarled, and elbowed Shura in the face.

Shura barely had time to be afraid. There was a white flash between his eyes, then a sharp pain. Something warm was spilling from his nose.

Suddenly the crowd erupted. A wave rushed through the throng as the entire street shouted, 'Hurrah! Hurrah!' The open-topped cars had just appeared at the very end of Nevsky Prospekt, down near the golden spire of the Admiralty building, carrying the returning heroes who made everyone so proud to be Soviet.

From inside the dense crowd, all Shura could see was backs and legs. Tears started streaming down his cheeks. Blood dripped on to his chin and his coat.

'Hey, boy, are you OK?' A man in a raincoat and a hat pushed a few people back with his arm to make space for Shura. 'Comrades, please! Be careful!' he said sternly. 'Are you savages? You've nearly crushed this poor boy!'

The surrounding people stepped aside slightly but didn't really take much notice. They were too busy shouting 'Hurrah!', impatiently standing on their tiptoes and waving their hats, scarves and newspapers in the air.

Sheltering Shura with one arm and edging his way through the crowd with the other, the man in the hat managed to drag Shura out of the crush.

'Oh dear me,' he muttered, pulling a handkerchief out of his pocket. The front of Shura's coat was splattered with blood.

'Look up,' said the man. With his glove still on, he scooped a handful of snow from the top of an iron bollard nearby, wrapped it in his handkerchief and pressed it against Shura's nose.

As Shura stood with his head tilted back, he saw a huge banner floating up above the crowd, bearing the portrait of a man with a moustache. Somewhere down below, beneath that banner, the famous polar explorer Papanin and his crew were driving past, followed by an exhilarated roar.

In bold yellow letters, the banner proclaimed: OUR LEADER AND ARCHITECT OF ALL OUR VICTORIES — OUR BELOVED COMRADE STALIN!

'I think it's stopped bleeding now,' the man in the hat reassured him, one eye on the banner. 'How did you manage to get a blow like that, comrade?'

Shura was devastated. He'd missed the parade!

'I'll get your hanky back to you,' Shura muttered. 'After Mama's washed it. Give me your address, so I can send it back.'

'Give you my address?' The man in the hat laughed kindly. 'Not likely!'

He aimed the scrunched-up bloody handkerchief at a cast-iron bin. It vanished inside.

Shura looked the stranger in the face. There was no sign that he was laughing at Shura. He looked a bit like Tanya's music teacher, only not quite so old.

'Do you know, I've a hankering for an ice cream. Since we missed the explorers, let's at least have an Eskimo in their honour,' the man said casually. 'Would you like an ice cream?'

'No, thank you,' said Shura, even though to have an Eskimo would be the best thing in world – nobody he knew had tried one yet! But then Shura realized that he perhaps wasn't being serious. 'Are you joking?'

'Me? I never joke.'

'Hmm . . . OK, then. Yes, please!'

They walked towards the corner of Nevsky Prospekt and Sadovaya Street – the corner with the two-storey wedge-shaped building, like a huge yellow-and-white iron. It was a department store that had been there since the days when there was a tsar in charge of the country, when Leningrad was called St Petersburg. Back then Gostiny Dvor had been an arcade full of private shops. Now the private businesses were gone and it had been turned into one big store for everyone. The pavement around it was covered by a colonnaded gallery, with white arches. There, beneath the vaulted ceiling, was an ice-cream man with a cart made of a blue box on large bicycle wheels.

Shura and the man in the hat walked over to the ice-cream vendor. Although it was March, the ice-cream man was wearing a fur hat with ears and white overalls over a quilted jacket. For him it was always winter, just as it was for the frosty goods he sold.

'Two Eskimos, please,' said the man in the hat.

'In honour of Comrade Papanin!' Shura exclaimed.

'In Comrade Papanin's honour! Then it's my treat,' said the ice-cream man with a smile, although he still took the money from the man in the hat.

He lifted the lid and disappeared for a second in the cloud of icy vapour, which burst from the box. When he resurfaced, he thrust into Shura's hand a chunky pole-shaped ice cream, chilly and wrapped in a marvellous silver paper.

'Let's go and sit down. It's not good for you to eat and walk at the same time,' said the man in the hat, unwrapping his ice cream with nimble fingers.

They walked to the public gardens by the theatre and sat on a bench. The cast-iron empress proudly held up her sceptre and her chin, entirely oblivious to the enormous water droplet hanging from the end of her nose and the pigeon squatting on her head. She looked extremely silly. Shura laughed.

The man in the hat gave him an inquiring look. But Shura just waved it off. It would take too long to explain! And, anyway, the pigeon flew off.

'So, how's your nose?' asked the man in the hat. 'Any better?'

Shura's nose hurt when he had to open his mouth wide to take a bite of ice cream, but he shook his head cheerfully. What a funny question! How could anything hurt when you're eating ice cream? And not just any ice cream but an Eskimo!

'It's fine,' Shura said. 'I didn't really need any help. I could have given him what for. Just didn't have time to . . .' He was devouring his ice cream, and his mouth was numb from the cold.

The man in the hat laughed. And then looked sad again.

'Of course you could have! It's just that my mother and father taught me to take the side of anyone who's being crushed by the crowd,' he explained.

The man in the hat seemed to be struggling to eat his Eskimo, as if it were cabbage soup or lumpy porridge and not ice cream. As though he had to force it down, as Mama would say. Shura felt a bit offended on behalf of the Eskimo; it deserved more appreciation. He smoothed out the wrapper from his, folded it and put it in his pocket.

'Did you know that the Eskimo was created in honour of the Soviet polar explorers?' said Shura. 'None of my friends have had one yet.'

The man in the hat gazed over at Nevsky Prospekt. The explorers had passed through. The marching band had finished playing. The police had allowed the traffic back on to the avenue: the cars started rumbling along at a rhythmic pace, the tram bells were ringing. But the hordes of people were still there. It was as though the convoy of heroes had gone past too quickly and the crowd still didn't want to go their separate ways.

'Just look at them,' said the man in the hat. 'Obsessed with the Arctic, the North Pole . . .' And then, out of the blue, he remarked, 'I can't see any healthy, ruddy cheeks. What have we got to be proud of? Building some kind of miraculous ice-breaker? Meanwhile their coats are in tatters and most of them left home without any breakfast.' The man shook his head. The ice cream was melting in his hand.

He's a funny fellow! thought Shura.

'Just look at them,' insisted the man.

Shura did as the man asked, just to be polite. Straight away he saw that the man was right: people looked happy, but their faces were long, weary and pale. And their clothes were old and tatty.

The man in the hat grew more animated. 'Did they ask this explorer, when they lifted him off that ice floe, if he wanted to be rescued? What if he didn't want to be brought back here? What if he got himself stuck there on purpose, to drift away from it all? Maybe he wanted to float away to some pretty little country, where people go for lovely winter strolls all wrapped up, cosy and warm, and come home and have hot chocolate and raisin buns.'

Shura gazed at him in alarm.

The man in the hat laughed. 'I'm joking. It's a fairy tale – the one about the Snow Queen! Do you want my Eskimo? Here. It's all yours!' He stood up. 'Enjoy it. Well, I'd better be off. A good day to you!' He tapped his fingers lightly on the brim of his hat, nodded to Shura, then set off in the direction of the theatre.

Shura hesitated a moment. But the Eskimo couldn't wait. His teeth hurt from the cold as he bit into the tube of ice cream, covered in delicious chocolate.

'So-o-o, what do we have here?' From behind him Shura heard a familiar smug, sing-song voice. 'Hanging about at Nevsky, are we? Caught red-handed! I'm telling Papa everything.'

Tanya did her annoying narrow-eyed stare at him, like she always did.

She was nine, only two years older than Shura. But she often acted like she thought she was nineteen. Or even ninety. Sometimes she'd chat to Shura and play with him just like any normal sister. But then sometimes it was like – snap! – she suddenly turned into the Evil Big Sister: horrid and fake, somehow.

'No need to pretend you're a grown-up, Tanya,' said Shura. He tried not to let it show that she had given him a fright, even though the shock made his tummy freeze, as though he'd gulped down the entire ice cream in one go.

Papa never told him off or shouted at him. He also never hit him, not like Valya's mama. She was a skinny woman who was always tired and grumpy. She would beat Valya with a leather belt or a towel, on his back, his legs or his bottom. But Shura's mama would simply hold her head in her hands in despair. Papa would just stare at him and say, 'How could this happen, Shura?' That was bad enough.

'Caught you! Messing around on Nevsky with Valya. Congr-r-r-ratulations!' Tanya sang, sarcastically trilling the 'r'.

'I'm not even with Valya, actually,' Shura snapped back. 'I'm here doing something important.'

'Oh, you are, are you?'

'Yes, actually.'

Tanya was carrying a pear-shaped case – her violin. She was on her way back from her music lesson. Her music teacher lived round the corner, on Sadovaya Street.

Shura cursed himself silently. How could he forget! He should have known there was a risk she'd spot him here in the gardens.

'Tanya, I wasn't messing around on Nevsky. I wanted to see Papanin and the polar explorers. You wouldn't understand.'

'Yeah, right!'

'You're just jealous.' Shura slowly and painstakingly licked the ice-cream stick clean.

Tanya watched his every move. She didn't need to be told that it was an Eskimo, the brand-new type of ice cream; that it was eye-wateringly expensive; and that none of the children on their street had had one yet.

Shura tossed the stick into the bin.

Tanya's eyes narrowed to slits again. 'I'm telling Mama and Papa.'

'Tell them; I don't care.'

'And I'm telling them you stole money for an ice cream.'

'Stole money!' Shura flushed hot, his face turned bright red.

'And who punched you in the nose?'

Shura remembered how he had got hit in the face when he was trying to catch a flyer for *her*! He felt so hurt he nearly cried.

'See! You're lying. You did steal it!' Tanya's voice rang in his ears. 'Valya taught you, didn't he? Mama and Papa will be so mad.'

'I didn't steal anything!'

'Did so!'

'Somebody bought me that ice cream, I'll have you know.'

'Oh yeah? Who – Papanin?' Shura couldn't bear how sarcastic his sister's voice was.

'Don't be stupid. A man.'

'You're lying,' she repeated.

'I'm not lying. He had a hat on.' Shura desperately looked around for the man.

'A man in a hat? And does he have a name?'

'I don't know. I've never met him before.'

'A total stranger bought you an ice cream? And you didn't even ask him his name to say thank you. Well, aren't you splendid! Did you hear that, citizens?'

'He did! He even gave me *his* Eskimo as well!'

Tanya's eyes suddenly burst wide. From narrow slits, they turned into two enormous green gooseberries. 'You've had *two*?'

'Yes. I've had two.' Shura looked at her defiantly. *Ha! Now what's she got to say to that?*

'Shura!'

Shura crossed his arms, a smug look on his face. Tanya stood there with her mouth hanging open, thunderstruck. *Serves her right*, thought Shura.

'Shura! You . . .?'

'That's right – I've had *two*,' he repeated proudly.

Tanya's case dropped to the ground with a thud.

'Shura!' Her face was serious now. She continued in a whisper: 'He must have been a foreign spy. An infiltrator!'

'Don't be silly!' Shura exclaimed, but inside it was like everything dropped. *An infiltrator?* The man had been a little strange – and those things he'd been saying about the explorers maybe not wanting to come back home because of how horrible it was here – well, that did sound like something an enemy of the state would say.

Shura picked up the violin case and brushed off the wet snow. He placed it on the bench for her, so Tanya would see that he was kind and good, unlike some people.

'What did he say to you?' Tanya sat down on the bench next to him. Shura could see from her face that she was genuinely worried. She wasn't pretending. Her tone of voice snuffed out Shura's confidence, like a bucket of water thrown on a bonfire.

'He said . . . er . . . that Papanin got stuck on the ice floe on purpose, to float off, far away from the Soviet Union.'

Tanya gasped. 'You see?'

Shura was cross with himself. No ordinary Soviet citizen would say something like that. He should never have spoken to a stranger – or taken an ice cream from him . . .

Now it all made sense. They warned them at school about spies and infiltrators. There were cases in the newspapers every day. There were constant reminders on the radio. Their parents talked about it at home. One had even been arrested at their father's office. Infiltrator. Saboteur. Spy.

Enemy of the People. And he, Shura, had just let one slip through his fingers.

He looked at his sister, terrified. 'Shall we go and find a policeman and tell him? I know! The ice-cream seller! He'll be able to describe him. Maybe I won't get in too much trouble – I *am* only seven.'

But Tanya didn't seem to be properly listening. 'The ice cream . . .' she whispered as she grabbed Shura by the shoulders. 'Shura . . . Did you definitely see him buy it?'

'Yes. I think so.' In his panic, Shura was struggling to remember exactly what had happened.

'What if he swapped it at the last moment?'

'Why would he do that?'

'It could have been poisoned!' Tanya was very close to his face now.

Shura did feel funny. *Poisoned!*

'How do you feel? Your stomach? Does it hurt?'

'No. Yes. I think so.' Shura forced the words out. His stomach was definitely churning.

'We need to call an ambulance, right away! Come on!' Tanya jumped up and grabbed her violin case.

'No!' Shura protested. He stayed sitting on the bench as thoughts went round and round his brain.

'What?'

'We shouldn't call an ambulance. Or get a policeman.'

'Why not?'

'Because I let the spy go. When he was saying the things about this not being a nice place, I didn't do anything. So the police won't help me – they'll arrest me!'

Tanya paused a moment to think. And then, unusually, she agreed with him. 'You're right,' she said slowly. 'But, so far, the only people who know about this are you and me.'

'And the ice-cream man,' Shura added anxiously.

'Never mind him.' Tanya was taking charge now. 'He probably assumed the man with the hat was your papa.'

Shura realized his stomach was still churning away with a funny knot in it. 'Tanya . . . Am I going to die?'

She didn't answer his question, but said, 'Let's get home quick. I know what to do!'

Shura couldn't quite believe that he might have let himself be poisoned, all for the sake of trying an Eskimo ice cream. Now he was going to die – just like that.

Tanya held his hand. 'Can you walk?'

Shura nodded, though he felt so peculiar now that he wasn't really sure he could.

When he stood, Shura's legs seemed to melt at the knees, but Tanya dragged him along behind her.

Closer to home, Tanya explained her idea. 'Do you remember when I ate that meat that had gone off? And Mama made me drink that pink stuff to make me sick until it was all out? That's what we need to do! We've still got some.'

Somehow or other, they managed to make it to the River Fontanka, along a backstreet towards the Five Corners junction and then there was their street with its good, reassuring Soviet name, Pravda Street – *Truth Street*. By now, Shura felt like he was burning inside.

They went up the stairs of their building and tiptoed down the long corridor. The huge flat they lived in had twelve rooms. Eleven families lived there, in one room each, except for Shura's family, who had two, the last ones on the corridor. Everyone shared the kitchen, where eleven tables lined the walls, and the corridor was also a space for everyone. They had to take it in turns to use the shared bathroom and toilet.

The light was gloomy. Nearly all of the rooms had their doors closed – like sleeping eyes, Shura thought. There was just one door where the faint sound of the gramophone could be heard. That was where an old woman lived, alone. She didn't go out to work, or anywhere really; the state paid her a pension. Shura often thought how lonely she must be.

Tanya pulled the door-key out from inside her coat; she kept it on a ribbon around her neck. She unlocked the door and everything was silent; Mama and Papa were at work and Bobka was at nursery.

They went straight into their main room – it was where Mama and Papa slept at night, but during the day the whole family used it. In the middle of the room was a large round table. That was where they ate, read, did their homework. Their parents' bed was behind a folding reed screen. Set against one wall was a large oak wardrobe.

Tanya opened the wardrobe door and walked into it, Shura following.

They were so used to doing this it didn't feel strange in any way. A long time ago, Papa had decided to link the two rooms together so they wouldn't have to go out into the corridor to get into their other room. He had knocked through to make a neat, rectangular doorway in the wall between the rooms, but then he hadn't been able to find a door the right size for it so he'd ended up covering the hole with an old wardrobe with the back taken off.

Shura loved that he had to shuffle through a wardrobe full of dresses and suits to get to his bedroom. Now, as he slipped through, a silky sleeve brushed his face, as though one of Mama's dresses were stroking him. For a moment it made him feel better, but then the feeling weighed heavily on his heart.

On the other side, Tanya helped Shura pull his boots off, get undressed and get into bed.

The wardrobe door creaked as Tanya disappeared again back into their parents' room on the way to the kitchen. Shura heard the door to the corridor bang. When he heard her come back, he imagined her pulling over a stool and rummaging in a box on the top shelf of the wardrobe, which the children were strictly forbidden from touching. But all Shura could hear was the gurgling inside his stomach.

Soon Tanya came back with a jug of warm water and the little bottle. She pulled out the rubber stopper and carefully shook a few dark-red crystals into the jug. The water immediately turned bright pink. 'Drink this,' she ordered.

From up close, her eyes seemed huge. Shura could see the brown speckles in her irises around the black pupils. They were like the freckles that there wasn't room for on Tanya's nose, Shura thought.

'Down in one!'

Shura obediently gulped it down. It felt like he had a glass ball inside his stomach.

Tanya went out and rushed back in with an empty saucepan.

'And now you need to puke into here! Come on!'

'I can't!'

'Come on, Shura – don't be stupid!'

'How do I make myself sick?'

'You need to stick your fingers in and tickle your tongue right at the back,' Tanya explained.

Shura did as he was told. His fingers fumbled around at the back of his throat. The glass ball inside him felt like it shuddered, crunched and gushed out as he vomited into the saucepan.

'Well done,' said Tanya. Shura couldn't remember when she'd last spoken to him so kindly. And she looked satisfied as she peered at the contents of the saucepan.

'What is it?' asked Shura, anxious in case she could see something terrible.

'You're safe now,' Tanya reassured him, picking up the saucepan.

Shura flopped back on to the pillow as Tanya took away the jug and the pan. He heard her go to the kitchen to wash them up. When she came back she dragged the stool away from the wardrobe to cover their tracks.

She wiped his mouth and the blood from his nose with a wet cloth. Then she felt Shura's forehead, just to check, like Mama always did when someone was poorly. She sat down next to him.

'Remember, Papa told us that there was a man at his work who was a spy and an enemy of the state, and they arrested

33

him. So, they'll catch your man in the hat, too. Don't worry. There's no place for vermin like that among good Soviet people. Now get some sleep. I need to go or I'll be late for school.'

'Don't leave me, Tanya!' Shura begged, suddenly afraid.

'I can't stay – otherwise they'll suspect something. Don't you see? Just act normal, like nothing happened. If Mama asks you, tell her you've got a sore throat. Say it's a cold. Got it?'

'Got it.'

'Repeat what I said.'

'I heard you!'

Tanya buttoned up her coat and grabbed her satchel. Shura heard the click as she left, locking the door behind her.

He lay in bed listening for any rumbles in his stomach, in case he hadn't managed to get rid of all the poison when he was sick. He didn't notice himself dozing off.

Maybe he had caught a chill when he was gulping down his freezing cold Eskimo ice cream because he struggled to wake up when Mama came in from work and was surprised to find him in bed.

'Oh, darling!' Mama threw off her coat and went to get him some food. She spoon-fed him some hot broth. His little brother stood quietly by the bed, his chin resting on his chubby little hands. Then Mama took Bobka with her, through the wardrobe, into the main room, leaving Shura to sleep a bit more.

Later on, Papa came home from work, too. He sat down by Shura's bed and felt his forehead with his soft, cool hand as Mama had done. 'Get well, little Shura,' he whispered. Shura was vaguely aware of his papa turning off the lamp on the bedside table.

Tanya came back. She gently poked him in the side.

All of this seemed to flicker in and out of Shura's consciousness, alternating with darkness. Then everything happened again, like the film reel starting over if you stay long enough at the cinema. Except this time it wasn't Papanin being paraded around in an open-topped car, with the crowd cheering ecstatically; it was the man in the hat. And there was a picture of the ice-cream seller on the huge banner next to Comrade Stalin, the leader of the Soviet nation. Comrade Stalin pointed at Shura in the crowd, wagging his finger and frowning at him.

Shura woke up. It was dark. A pale patch of light – maybe the moonlight, or maybe the street lamp – shone on his sister's face as she slept, her two plaits stretching down either side of her head.

'Tanya!' Shura whispered.

His sister didn't answer.

Fine, let her sleep, he thought. He listened out for any murmurs inside his tummy. Nothing. Did that mean Tanya's trick had worked? Or, perhaps, the opposite: his time was up? Perhaps he wasn't simply lying in bed, but was slowly dying?

The thought sent a shiver down his spine.

However, he was glad to have bumped into Tanya after

the parade; she had kept a cool head. Shura thought he had better leave his pencils to her if he did die. And his brand-new drawing set, the one he had got in September when he started school. He suddenly desperately wanted to wake her up to say goodbye.

'Tanya!' he called again. But his sister only frowned a little, before her forehead smoothed over again in the moonlight.

Well, sleep then, you idiot, thought Shura, cross that he might die here alone.

But it's all your own fault, he told himself. How many times had he heard at school and on the radio: *Be careful – the walls have ears; there may be a spy and an enemy among us.*

Shura sighed bitterly. What a waste of seven years! There was so much he hadn't done; he'd never even owned a dog. And now this pointless end. And all because he wanted to try the new Eskimo before the rest of the kids in their yard. How stupid!

If only he had gone to Nevsky with Valya and hadn't been alone! If only Valya hadn't thrown that brick at Auntie Dusya's window! If only they hadn't argued over that stupid note that had ruined everything!

Valya is sure to cry at my funeral. And so will Auntie Dusya. And Mama and Papa, of course. But it'll be too late.

Shura's eyes started to fill with tears.

Suddenly he heard muffled but stern voices on the other side of the wardrobe. Mama. Papa. Somebody else. Someone familiar. Bobka started to whine. He was sleeping in their parents' room tonight because of Shura being poorly. The voices rumbled on.

Shura sniffed. He listened as hard as he could. But it wasn't long before he was fast asleep again . . .

He finally woke up properly to the steady drip-drip on the windowsill. A flurry of drips broke the rhythm, but then it settled down again. The sun had painted a large bright square on the shiny floor and was quietly admiring its work.

I'm alive! Shura sat up in his bed, ecstatic. *It worked!*

His sister's bed was empty. It seemed odd that nobody had woken him up for school. They probably thought he was still poorly. *But I'm alive*, he rejoiced. *And life is fantastic!*

Breakfast was probably waiting for him on the table, he thought. Pancakes or porridge. Or maybe fried eggs. Hmmm. Licking his lips at the thought of delicious, hot fried eggs, Shura slipped out of bed and walked, barefoot, over to the wardrobe. *I'll go quietly and give them a nice surprise*, he thought, picturing his family sitting at the table.

He shuffled through the dresses and suits in the wardrobe.

He flung open the wardrobe door.

Instead of breakfast on the table, there was a large bowl and in it flickered a small orange flame. Mama was furiously tearing up sheets of paper and feeding the tiny shreds to the flame one by one; she didn't even notice him enter the room.

Tanya stared at Shura, wide-eyed. She didn't look happy to see him or surprised. She just looked scared.

Papa wasn't there.

Neither was Bobka.

Mama now started shredding photographs.

'Tanya, help me, please!' There was desperation in her voice. She nudged a heap of papers across the table to her.

Tanya held an entire sheet of paper over the flame, which licked at it with its long tongue.

'No! Rip them up first! Little pieces!' Mama exclaimed. 'The last thing we need is for the neighbours to come running in because they can smell the smoke!'

'Mama!' Shura called, afraid.

'Oh, Shura! You're awake!' Mama tried to look pleased, but Shura could tell she wasn't pleased – her lips just twisted upward a tiny bit.

She started to dash around the room. She pulled a large pair of felt boots and an old blanket out of the wardrobe and tossed them on to a heap of clothes.

'How are you feeling?' Mama asked, but she didn't stop to hear the answer as she hurried past Shura carrying the pile of clothes. Tanya glared at him – she seemed to be trying to tell him something with her facial expression.

'Fine,' Shura murmured softly. His face suddenly burned with shame as he remembered Tanya giving him the medicine to make him sick yesterday.

Luckily, Mama didn't seem to have noticed anything. She was piling the clothes into a small plywood suitcase. She even threw in thick woollen socks and an old woollen waistcoat, one that she always said needed to be thrown out.

'Where's Bobka?' asked Shura.

Mama didn't seem to hear the question. She was staring distractedly at the suitcase, which stood before her with its mouth gaping open.

Tanya answered instead. 'He's at nursery. Where else would he be?'

'Mama, don't I have to go to school today?' asked Shura.

'What?' Mama said, suddenly aware of him again. 'Of course, you do! If you're feeling better,' she added more warmly.

'I —'

But Mama didn't let him finish. Her thoughts were elsewhere already.

'Of course. Definitely. Have some bread and milk, will you? I haven't made any breakfast. Look in the cupboard.'

'The old woman will shout at me for being late.'

'Don't call her that — she's your teacher. And she won't tell you off because I'll write a note for you to take. OK?'

Shura nodded.

'And where's Papa?'

'He's gone away,' Mama said quickly. 'He's gone away. Not for long. He had to go on an urgent business trip. They sent a telegram and asked him to come. So he had to go away for a bit. But he'll be back soon. Definitely. They'll sort it all out and he'll be back soon.'

Mama carried on dashing back and forth between the wardrobe and the suitcase. Tanya watched her with huge round eyes.

'A special one?' asked Shura.

'What?' said Mama.

'Is it a special business trip?'

'Yes, it's important,' Mama said with a sigh.

'Where to?' Shura asked.

Amazing! he thought. *Papa's been called away on a business trip! Maybe he's gone to the Urals or Siberia to work on a very important Soviet construction project!*

'Where's Papa gone?' he asked again.

'Will you please stop asking?' Mama suddenly shouted. 'Where! Where! Where! First one! Now the other! Can't you just stop pestering me!' She stopped. She let go of the hat she was holding and burst into tears.

'Mama!' Tanya ran up and put her arms around her.

Shura burst into tears, too. Everything felt so confusing. Mama knelt down in front of him and gave him a hug.

'It's OK, it's OK, it's going to be all right,' she muttered, stroking Shura's back with one hand and Tanya's hands with the other. 'Oh, aren't we silly? All of us sobbing like this. It's a good thing Bobka's not here; he wouldn't know whether to laugh or cry. Papa will be back soon, OK. Don't worry, Tanya. Shura? OK? Good girl. Good boy.'

Mama stood up and wiped her tears with the back of her hand. 'Come on, Shura – wash your face and off you go to school. If you're any later, people will talk, darling. It's wonderful that Papa has been asked to go on this trip. We should be very proud of him.'

Within minutes Shura was dressed and ready to go, holding a slice of bread in one hand and throwing his satchel on to his shoulder with the other as he stepped out of the door.

In the corridor, their neighbour Auntie Rita stared at him. Her head was full of hair curlers.

'Good morning!' Shura called out cheerfully.

But she didn't answer.

'My papa's gone away on a business trip! He was called urgently!' he announced proudly, excited to tell everyone.

Auntie Rita must have been very surprised, as her mouth dropped open. *Well, let her stand and gawp, the silly thing*, thought Shura.

Another neighbour, the old woman who didn't go out to work, and who nobody was friends with, came the other way down the corridor towards the shared bathroom.

'Morning, Shura,' she mumbled, looking at the floor as she scurried past.

Shura gave a resounding 'Good morning!'

'You might be best to keep away from other people's children!' Auntie Rita shouted to her. 'You never know . . .' She stopped.

'Never know what?' asked the old woman.

Shura opened the door to the stairs. And, as he did so, he heard Auntie Rita whisper something so strange that he presumed he had misheard it.

'The Black Raven came for our neighbour last night.'

CHAPTER THREE

'A black raven? Came and took Papa away?' Tanya snorted. 'Don't be ridiculous. Papa's gone away on business, Mama said. Didn't you hear her?'

All morning at school, Shura had been eager to get home, impatiently waiting for the bell to go. He checked the classroom clock constantly, but the black hands crept round so slowly that he kept thinking they must be stuck. He couldn't wait to tell Tanya what he'd heard about the black raven. Could it be true that a raven had taken Papa? He was dying to talk to her about it. Even the breaks between the lessons seemed to drag on longer than a maths lesson.

As he walked home along the River Fontanka, the road felt never-ending; other people seemed determined to get in his way, and the pedestrian lights at the crossing took forever to change to green.

Finally, he got home and could blurt everything out that he'd been so desperate to tell Tanya. But all she had to say was, 'Don't be ridiculous.'

She pulled a stool over the window.

'I heard it myself!'

'Yeah, from our gossipy neighbour,' Tanya reminded him.

'That's what I said.'

'From Auntie Rita.'

'Yes, that's what I said!'

'*That's what I said!*' Tanya mimicked him. 'And babies are delivered by a stork and bread rolls grow on trees and the moon is made of cheese. Don't you see? They think you're a baby, so they know you'll believe all sorts of nonsense.'

'I'm not a baby,' Shura objected.

'Auntie Rita's not exactly the most reliable person, is she?' said Tanya. 'She's got hair curlers for a brain. She blathers on just for the sake of talking. And she's *petit bourgeois*. Don't you see?'

He knew it wasn't good to be *petit bourgeois*. Shura had heard Mama and Papa say so, although he wasn't really sure what it meant.

Tanya stepped on to the stool and then stood up on the windowsill. She opened the small ventilation window and stretched out her skinny arm and dropped some breadcrumbs on to the little wooden bird feeder hanging outside. They always put food out for the birds over the winter.

Tanya closed the window but stayed standing on the windowsill for a moment, waiting to see if any birds flew over.

'Isn't it odd?' she said quietly as she looked through the cold glass. 'People are almost the only animals that don't hibernate in winter, so it's good that there are still a few birds about to keep us company.'

A sparrow landed on the feeder, balancing on its scrawny little legs, and started pecking at the crumbs. Tanya and Shura watched it in silence for a little while.

But Shura couldn't get the image of a black raven taking Papa out of his head. 'We need to save Papa,' he insisted.

Tanya took her time to climb down.

'If we did need to save Papa, Mama wouldn't have taken Bobka to nursery, would she?' Tanya explained patiently. 'And she wouldn't have gone to work. Mama said he had to go on an urgent business trip. Why would she lie? Anyway, I have to pack my bag for school this afternoon. And we still need to have lunch. Why don't you lay the table?'

She didn't seem troubled in the slightest by Shura's version of events, and Shura also started to wonder if he'd been getting worked up about nothing.

Tanya straightened the curtains.

With the gentle blue sky outside the window, Auntie Rita's words no longer seemed so sinister. Tanya was probably right, Shura thought. But he still stuck his tongue out at her.

Tanya cleared her school books from the table and shoved them into her satchel. She smoothed out the tablecloth. Shura laid out two soup bowls and two spoons.

Usually, Mama didn't come back from work until the evening and Bobka stayed late at nursery. Shura and Tanya normally had lunch together at home, after Shura got back from school and before Tanya went.

Tanya carefully unravelled the blanket that was swaddled around the saucepan of soup that their mama had left them. Mama always cooked something and wrapped it up like this before she went to work. The pan was still warm.

Suddenly they heard a key unlocking the door.

'Mama?'

Mama came in, pulled off her boots and hung up her coat.

'Mama! Hurrah!' Shura ran up and threw his arms around her.

'You're home for lunch?' Tanya was surprised.

'Yes, and no. I'm not going back.'

Shura skipped over to the cupboard to get another bowl. He stopped halfway. 'What about Bobka?'

'I'll pick Bobka up later,' Mama said softly. 'Oh, isn't this lovely?' she said, inspecting the table the children had laid. 'I'm lucky to be able to have lunch with you for a change!'

They sat down to a meal of soup followed by meatballs. Mama was silent as she ate, and Tanya and Shura were quiet, too. Then she poured some tea for the children and coffee for herself. Again, not a word.

'Mama, are you poorly?' Shura asked eventually.

'No, I'm fine,' said Mama in a chirpy voice. She sipped her coffee.

Shura suddenly thought of a time when they were in a shop buying china teacups. The shop assistant tapped lightly on each cup with a pencil to show the ringing sound they made – that meant there were no cracks in the cup. But one of them made a different sound, because it had an invisible crack. They replaced it with a new cup, with the proper, clear ring. That's how it was with Mama's 'No, I'm fine': her voice didn't have quite the right ring. As though there were an invisible crack.

Tanya also seemed to have pricked up her ears. They both looked at Mama inquisitively.

'Do you know what? I'm actually fed up of my job,' Mama announced.

'What do you mean?' Tanya asked, suspicious.

'Well, you don't always want to go to school, do you?' Shura laughed.

'Well, I've had enough of this job. I'll find another one.' Mama shook her head nonchalantly and started stirring some sugar into her coffee. The more she stirred, the more her spoon knocked against the sides of the cup. The coffee whirled around and splashed over the edge. A brown patch started to spread on the tablecloth.

'Mama, what are you doing?' Tanya cried.

She kept stirring and the spoon kept knocking the sides with a *ting*, *ting*, *ting*.

'Mama!'

Mama looked at the cup as if she had just woken up. Then she looked at the children who were watching her, not knowing what to say.

'Oh, don't worry,' she said, and placed a paper napkin over the coffee stain. 'I've just had a splendid idea,' she added, changing the subject. 'Tanya can skip school this afternoon. We'll all stay at home and read a book together. How does that sound?'

'Yeah!' cried Shura. 'Or we could go to the cinema?'

'Or we could go to the cinema!' Mama echoed. Then she looked at Tanya, who hadn't said a word. 'Tanya, why so serious? Would you rather go to school?'

'No.'

Tanya did look serious, suspicious even. Shura looked at

his sister and his mama. It seemed like Mama was somehow *too* happy. Was it possible to be *too* happy about something? Well, either way, he was certainly happy about Mama's idea.

'And then we'll all go together to collect Bobka. That'll be a nice surprise for him!'

'Hurrah!' shouted Shura.

So they stayed at home that afternoon and read books. Then they collected Bobka from nursery. He was surprised to see his brother and sister with Mama and loved skipping home holding hands with them.

They played cards and bingo. Bobka tried to join in with bingo, although he didn't know the numbers yet. Shura showed him where to place the counters to cover up the numbers. Bobka proudly held a handful of counters in his little chubby fist.

Eventually Bobka started blinking and yawning sleepily.

'It's someone's bedtime, isn't it?' Mama laughed, giving Bobka a kiss. She started to help him out of his breeches, then pulled off his stockings.

'What about his cot?' asked Tanya. She glanced at Shura.

Last night, when Shura was 'poorly', his parents had moved Bobka's cot into their room. But because Papa had been called away urgently he hadn't had time to move Bobka's cot back into the children's room.

Shura blushed. He couldn't bear even to think about yesterday: the man in the hat, the ice cream, the medicine, being sick . . . But he wasn't quite sure why it all made him feel so strange.

Bobka clung to the bars of his cot.

'We'll help! We can move it back,' Shura suggested.

'No, don't worry. He can sleep here with me. You two go through to your room. I'll come and join you in a bit.'

Tanya and Shura squeezed through the wardrobe, back to their bedroom. Then Mama came and joined them, and they read some more. Mama had never read to them as much as she did that day. Her voice sounded so lovely, so calm.

Tanya seemed to relax. And Shura's mind was put at rest.

'OK, time for everyone to go to sleep,' said Mama. She clapped the book shut.

Lying in bed in the dark, Shura couldn't stop his mind from going back to what their neighbour had said about the black raven. He stared at the murky yellow rectangle of light on the floor from the street lamp or perhaps from the moon.

'Tanya, what does *petit bourgeois* mean?' asked Shura.

'Mmm?' She raised her head from the pillow to hear him.

'And why would Auntie Rita make up stories about where Papa is?'

'Well, when you're a *petit bourgeois*, you want another sofa even when you've already got one,' explained Tanya.

'What's that got to do with Papa?'

'Nothing – it's just how Auntie Rita is.'

'How?'

'Hey, you two!' Mama called from the other room. 'Enough chatting! Time to go to sleep.'

'Papa says that she's never content with what she's got and she envies everyone else,' Tanya whispered, shuffling around and kicking her feet until her blanket was tucked under her, covering her shoulders and her toes.

Shura closed his eyes . . . When he opened them again, he found himself in a long corridor. Walking slowly and silently towards him was a woman with a giant crow's beak. He felt sure that it was Auntie Rita. But at the same time it was the Black Raven.

Terrified, Shura started slapping himself in the face. *Phew, it doesn't hurt. That means this is only a dream.*

He ran and ran – but his movements were slow and difficult, in that way that running always feels like you're caught in a spider's web when you're dreaming. The corridor never seemed to end. He could hear muffled voices on the other side of the wall. Bobka was whimpering.

'That's just a wardrobe.' His mama's voice suddenly penetrated into his dream, sounding unusually loud and distinct. There was a dull thud on the spare door to the children's room, the one that went through to the corridor. Another knock, then a few moments later footsteps walking away.

More voices.

Their parents' door slammed shut.

'The Black Raven,' he distinctly heard Auntie Rita say. It sounded like she was savouring the words.

Shura opened his eyes again. A pale rectangle of light trembled on the ceiling. Outside, he could hear the rumble of an engine running. Tanya was asleep.

'Get back inside!' he heard Auntie Rita bossing someone around in the corridor. 'Nothing to see here. It was the neighbours in the far room.'

Another door creaked open. Muttering.

'Who was it? Who was it?'

'The Black Raven. They've just gone.'

The Raven? Shura sat bolt upright.

'Tanya!' He leapt out of bed and started shaking his sister to wake her up, whispering right into her ear. 'Tanya! The Black Raven! He was here! Just now!'

Shura dashed to the window and brushed the curtain aside. He pulled himself up on to the windowsill and pressed his forehead against the cold glass to get a good view of the whole street.

Straight below he could see the square roof of a large car – a black car, with nothing special about it. The street lights were still on. All the windows in the street were dark. The street was completely empty. Except there was Petrovich, the old caretaker, leaning his arms on his shovel. He was dressed in only his long johns and a shirt, with a sheepskin coat draped over his shoulders. The light from the street lamp glinted on his bald patch.

'Where? Let me see. Don't push!' Tanya peered out of the window, turning her head from side to side trying to see.

'He was just here! I heard!'

'Shhh! You'll wake up Mama and Bobka!'

A stooped figure was led quickly out of the building by two other people. The three of them ducked to climb inside the car.

The car doors slammed shut, the engine gave a throaty roar and the headlights lit up the mucky March snow.

The rectangle of light on the children's ceiling slanted to

the side, then slid down the wall and disappeared. The rumble of the engine slowly dwindled away into the damp night.

Petrovich, who looked short and dumpy from above, wrapped his sheepskin tighter around himself. He stood there for a while. Then he started scraping the snow with the shovel, dragging the slush about and trampling it down. Soon there was no longer any trace of the black car's tyre marks. And then the caretaker went back inside the building.

'Get down from the windowsill, quick, before Mama wakes up,' Tanya whispered, pulling the hem of Shura's pyjamas.

'I'm telling you, that was the Black Raven,' Shura whispered.

'We didn't see anything!'

'We were too late,' said Shura, annoyed. 'But I heard! Someone in the corridor definitely said "Black Raven".'

'Auntie Rita again, by any chance?'

'Not just her.'

Tanya thought for a moment. 'Well, it can't be true,' she said, straightening out her blanket.

'Tomorrow, let's tell Mama everything.'

'Everything?' Tanya stopped, with her blanket in her hands.

'Yes, and about the spy I met, and him maybe poisoning me. Honesty is the best policy.'

'Don't even think about it! I risked everything to get that pink medicine for you!'

Shura gave a loud sigh.

'Shhh,' Tanya whispered. 'Bobka.'

They listened for a while. All was quiet.

'Be grateful we didn't wake up Bobka,' Tanya whispered. 'Don't you dare tell her anything without me. Do you hear? Only if we do it together.'

Shura promised.

Then they talked a little about what they'd tell Mama tomorrow, and what they wouldn't mention. And what Papa would say if he found out. But their thoughts became sluggish and confused, and before they'd managed to agree on what they were going to say they'd both drifted off to sleep.

Shura woke up first. He needed the toilet. But he remembered that he'd promised Tanya he wouldn't go through to their parents' room without her. So he stuck his hand under her blanket and poked Tanya in the side, then quickly hid under his blanket and turned to face the wall.

'No point pretending that wasn't you,' Tanya said in her patronizing voice. 'I wasn't asleep. I've been thinking.'

She pulled Shura's blanket off him. He got out of bed and put his bare feet on the floor.

'Ooh, it's cold. Hasn't Mama done the fire?'

Tanya shrugged.

They padded across the cold floor to the wardrobe. On the other side, they flung the door open.

It was eerily quiet in their parents' room. The clock had stopped, the kettle was cold, and so was the stove. Mama wasn't there. Bobka's cot was empty. Mama's boots, coat, gloves, hat and shawl were all gone. The suitcase wasn't there. Bobka's coat, hat, scarf and felt boots had all vanished, too. Only his tiny mittens, joined together on a long elastic thread so that he didn't lose them – or lost both at once – were hanging on the hook.

Tanya took them down and stared at them as if she had never seen them before. The floor was scattered with photograph albums, the ones Mama had been tearing pictures out of and feeding to the fire yesterday. They lay open with empty pages sticking up in the air helplessly. Things were strewn around as if someone had picked the whole room up, turned it upside down, shaken everything out and then dropped it back down.

'Well, I never,' said Tanya.

Shura stared at the mittens, then at Tanya.

'What?' asked Tanya. 'Mama's probably gone to work – that's all.'

'But she said she'd quit her job.'

'She said she'd find another one!'

'What about Bobka?'

'He's at nursery. Where else would he be?'

Someone was knocking softly at the door.

Tanya ran over and opened it. Shura followed her, curious. The old woman from down the hall stood there, blinking nervously. The light glinted dimly on the bicycle leaning against the wall behind her, and behind that was the dark shape of an old chest. The neighbours tended to leave items they didn't need every day in the shared corridor.

'Hello . . . What do you want?' Tanya asked, surprised to see her.

Glancing back towards the other end of the corridor, where the communal kitchen was, the old woman offered Tanya a little purse with a button.

'Your mother asked me to give you this,' she whispered. 'And she said you should go to your aunt's.'

Shura noticed for the first time that the old woman had blue eyes. He had never had a chance to see her face properly before: she usually scuttled like a mouse along the corridor into the kitchen and bathroom. She tried to keep out of everyone's way.

'And where is Mama?' Tanya asked.

But the woman dropped the purse on the floor and scurried away down the long corridor back to her room.

'What a funny lady.' Tanya picked up the purse.

She locked the door and they had a look inside. The purse contained over a hundred roubles.

'Wow!' Shura gasped. 'Why has Mama given us so much money?'

'We need to go to Auntie Vera's.'

'Why?'

'Because that's what the old lady said. Mama told her that we should go to our aunt's.'

Auntie Vera was Mama's sister, and she lived over on Kamenny Island. You needed to take a tram across the River Neva to get there. From her place, you could see the fortress to the right, that reddish-brown building that looked like it was built out of gingerbread, with a tall golden spire on top. And, to the

54

left, the gleaming domes of the mosque sparkled through the trees, their sky-blue colour competing with the sky itself.

'And this is the money for the tram,' Tanya concluded.

'Isn't it a bit much for a tram?'

Auntie Vera was a strange lady. Her flat was absolutely full of books and paintings, brushes and tubes of paint – on the shelves, on the surfaces, on the floor – and there was a funny smell. She didn't have any children and she lived on her own.

'Mama said go to Auntie Vera's, so come on – we'd better go,' said Tanya. 'Let's get ready.'

They both hated going to Auntie Vera's. But what could they do? It was odd their mother hadn't told them herself, but she had left clear instructions.

'But, Tanya, the old woman might have got it wrong.'

'Don't be silly.'

'But listen!' Shura insisted. 'Mama probably said, ". . . and if they want, they can go to Auntie Vera's." It's just that the old woman forgot the "if they want" bit.'

Tanya looked at her brother, seriously contemplating the idea. She didn't want to go to Auntie Vera's either. She was a tall, stern woman, with a long nose and cold grey eyes. Auntie Vera never smiled. It was hard to believe that she was Mama's sister.

Shura could see that Tanya was quite taken by this possibility.

'Tanya, just think about it. It's obvious. Remember yesterday Mama said we didn't have to go to school and could play at home all day? Well, I bet she wants us to have fun today, too. We don't have to go to school. We can do what we want!'

Tanya thought for a moment.

'And she left us some money for ice cream!' added Shura, with a huge grin.

'Ice cream . . .! You should be grateful I didn't tell her yesterday what you'd been up to at Nevsky Prospekt.'

But Shura wasn't in the mood to give in. 'And we could go to the movies! And buy sweets! There's even enough to buy a toy!'

Tanya looked at the purse: it really was stuffed full.

'Why would Mama do that?' she wondered, still sounding doubtful. 'It's not anyone's birthday or New Year.'

But Shura saw a little flame flicker in her eyes.

'Because she's our mama – that's why! The best mama in the world!' He grabbed Tanya's hands. 'So? Shall we run into town?'

Tanya finally gave in. 'Hmm, OK then. Let's go. But we'll walk – not run,' she added, in a bossy tone of voice.

'Hurrah!' cried Shura. He leapt on to the sofa and started bouncing so much that the springs squeaked. 'Hurrah! De-de-de-daa! The best mama in the world!'

CHAPTER FOUR

They decided they should have some breakfast before going out. But they weren't allowed to use matches, so they couldn't light the portable stove to put the kettle on.

'I'll ask one of the neighbours. Shura, can you slice some bread?' said Tanya, taking the kettle with her as she left the room.

The communal kitchen was always busy in the mornings: people making breakfast, Auntie Rita heating her curlers, someone doing their laundry, someone else washing up.

Tanya came back almost immediately. All Shura had managed to do was take the bread out of the bread bin.

'Everyone's acting a bit strange today,' Tanya said. 'No one would help me. It was like they couldn't see me or hear me.'

'Oh, so, can't we have tea? That's a shame.' His stomach was rumbling.

Tanya paused to think. 'I know what we should do.' She waved the purse. 'Let's have breakfast at the Nord! We'll have éclairs and *bouche* cream puffs and hot chocolate. And we can even buy a box of little treats to bring home for Mama and Bobka!'

The Nord was the best cafe in all of Leningrad. It had huge windows facing Nevsky Prospekt, with white china figurines of bears on display. There were glass tabletops, and the waitresses wore little lacy bonnets. Tanya and Shura only ever went to the Nord on their birthdays.

'Ooh, yes!' Shura exclaimed.

'But we should tidy up first,' said Tanya. 'Mama overslept and was running late for work. She's left stuff scattered everywhere, she was in such a rush. She'll be so pleased when she comes back and sees that we've tidied up.'

'Good idea!' said Shura. He picked up a chair and dragged it over to the wall. On the way, he picked a book up from the floor.

Tanya started putting away the photograph albums. Then she carefully gathered and folded up all the clothes.

They kept going, motivated by the prospect of the green sofas, cream puffs, éclairs, hot chocolate, and everything that the Nord was famous for.

At last, Tanya said, 'OK, that'll do. Let's go.'

They quickly put their coats on. At the door, they cast a final glance at their hard work: their parents' room looked 'spick and span', as Papa would say. They stomped cheerfully down the stairs and ran out into the street.

It was already light outside; the sun was up. The caretaker was sprinkling sand over the icy pavements. Tanya carefully checked the ground with one foot before stepping on it properly; it was slippery.

'Morning!' cried Shura. 'Proper spring weather! Warm in the day, but still freezing at night. That's what Mama always says.'

The caretaker stopped and gave them a quizzical look as they walked past. Then he started scattering handfuls of sand again.

Shura turned to look back at their windows, like he always did. The glass reflected the bright-blue sky. He noticed Auntie Dusya's face in one of the ground-floor windows. He smiled at her, but she frowned and pulled the curtains across. She was probably still angry about the broken glass.

At the crossing, Tanya suddenly stopped. 'Listen, I'm starving. Let's have a pasty. I can't last till the cafe!'

There was a street vendor on the corner with a box of pasties, covered with a thick blanket to keep them warm. As soon as Shura smelt the deep-fried *pirozhki*, his stomach started growling, like an orchestra bursting into action.

'Oh yes, let's start with a pasty!' shouted Shura, as he ran over to the vendor. 'Can I please have one of your delicious ones with jam?' he asked.

'Have you got any money?' asked the vendor frostily. Her white apron was covered in greasy spots.

People walked past in a hurry.

'Two with jam, please,' Tanya said, handing her the right change.

The vendor gave her two pasties wrapped in parchment paper. Tanya passed one to her brother.

As they walked, Shura sank his teeth into the pastry, and hot strawberry jam oozed out of the other end. Shura let a giggle of delight: a *pirozhok* first thing in the morning, and no school!

As the ice melted on the roofs, the houses dripped large,

chilly water drops that sparkled like diamonds in the sun. A flock of pigeons swooped up with a great flap and fluttered away over the houses, their coloured feathers glinting in the sunlight.

'So, shall we go to the cinema, then? There's a morning showing at the Aurora,' Tanya suggested dreamily.

'Um, Tanya,' said Shura, licking jam from the palm of his hand and running to catch up with his sister. 'How about we find the Black Raven first, who's taken Papa? Imagine how happy Mama will be when she gets home and sees we've found him. She'll be so pleased.'

Tanya rolled her eyes and sighed. Not rushing to reply, she slowly wiped her lips with the edge of the paper the *pirozhok* had been wrapped in.

'What?' Shura said.

'Enough of that nonsense. It's not funny.'

'It's not nonsense! It's what I heard.'

Tanya gave his hand a tug. 'Come on! Let's go – or we'll miss the start of the film.'

'That means you don't love Papa!' yelled Shura.

'I don't love Papa?' Tanya's face turned flaming red. 'Oh, for goodness' sake! Fine, shall we go up and ask someone about this Black Raven who supposedly comes along and carries people off in the night? Let's go and see if they don't just laugh at us! Then see how you feel. Who are you going to believe? Will you believe a policeman? Come on, then – we'll go and find a policeman.'

They walked the entire length of Vladimirsky Prospekt. The pedestrians walked mainly on the sunny side of the street. Cars trundled past.

Finally, on the corner of Nevsky Prospekt, they saw a policeman on duty, directing the traffic. In his white helmet and gloves, with a black holster stretched across his chest, he was gesticulating like a conductor to an orchestra. As he held up a hand to signal, one lane of traffic would stop and the other would go.

'Comrade Policeman!' Tanya called out and waved to him.

'Wait, Tanya!' said Shura, suddenly anxious in case the Black Raven story was a load of nonsense after all. 'We don't need to bother the policeman!'

'Yes, we do,' Tanya insisted. 'Let's go and sort it out once and for all, so I don't have to listen to your idiotic stories all day long.'

The policeman came over to them with a haughty stride. He touched his hand to the side of his helmet in salute.

'Good day, children. How can I help?'

Shura couldn't utter a word.

'Good day to you, Comrade Policeman!' Tanya spoke boldly.

'Are you lost?' asked the policeman.

'Oh no, not at all! We know our way around. We even know the Highway Code!' Tanya smiled politely, to show off her good manners.

Shura gave her a little kick.

'May we ask you a question, please, Comrade Policeman?' Tanya asked in her sweetest voice, like a good little girl.

'Of course,' the policeman replied, beaming broadly. He bent down slightly. He had a very kindly face. When he smiled, his rosy cheeks bulged out like two red apples.

Tanya tried to look as grown-up as she could, which made Shura want to kick her again, even harder. 'This little boy wants to ask you something. It's rather silly, to be honest.'

Shura tugged on Tanya's plait. The policeman laughed.

'I'm all ears, my friend.' He crouched in front of Shura. 'What did you want to ask? I'll answer as best I can.'

Shura was reassured by how the policeman was taking him seriously and speaking to him like a grown-up. Feeling bolder, he started to explain. 'Comrade Policeman, my papa was taken away by the Black Raven –'

'You're surely going to laugh,' Tanya interrupted, but quickly broke off.

The kindly policeman didn't laugh at all. His smile completely vanished from his face. The colour drained from his rosy apple cheeks. Even his lips turned grey. Very slowly, the policeman stood up. His eyes darted around.

'Run!' squealed Tanya, yanking Shura by the hand. They dashed across the road, towards Liteiny Prospekt.

'Stop!' yelled the policeman.

Shura could barely keep up with his sister. But the policeman's reaction told him that she'd been right to run.

Tanya darted into an archway off the street into a courtyard. They knew their way; this block had three inner courtyards, each joined with an arch beneath the building. It would take them through to the River Fontanka on the other side. Tanya and Shura ran through the first courtyard.

Behind them, they heard a voice shout 'This way!' followed by the thud of the policeman's boots echoing beneath the archway.

The next arch was blocked by a padlocked gate. Tanya and Shura wriggled their way through the bars, managing to squeeze through just in time. They carried on running at full pelt. Ahead of them, through the final archway, they could see the water lapping at the granite river embankment, with its decorative iron railings.

The policeman shook the gate in frustrated anger. The gaps between the bars were too small for a grown man to climb through.

'Caretaker!' he shouted, banging his fists on the gate. The iron bars rang out loudly. 'Why are the gates locked in the day?'

Shura and Tanya didn't hear the rest. They kept running along the embankment and over the bridge, towards the big junction where the main roads met.

'Shura, don't stop!' shouted Tanya, gasping for air as she ran.

By the time they reached the junction, they realized they weren't being followed any more. Tanya slowed down. Her legs were shaking. Shura took some deep breaths, panting more out of fear than exhaustion. He had been in plenty of scrapes with Valya, after all. They'd had caretakers shooing them, people shouting at them. But to be chased by a policeman? Like a criminal? This was a first!

Shura swiped his cap off his head and used it to wipe his face, which was streaming sweat. He sat down on a stone bollard next to one of the huge buildings. It was where people used to tie up their horses in the olden days.

Tanya looked at him and suddenly burst out laughing. 'What a dunce! Did you see his face?'

Shura couldn't help but laugh, too. 'And did you hear his boots stomping when he ran?' He giggled as he remembered the policeman jumping about, shouting and banging the gate.

Tanya doubled over with laughter. 'Oh, my stomach hurts from laughing!'

Then Shura suddenly turned deadly serious as something dawned on him. 'Tanya . . . Tanya!'

'What?' asked his sister, wiping away her hysterical tears.

'Tanya, the way the policeman reacted . . . it means the Black Raven must be real.'

She didn't say anything. Her smile faded.

'He *does* exist, Tanya. The policeman knew what I was talking about.'

Tanya removed a mitten. She snapped an icicle off one of the windowsills and popped it in her mouth.

'And it's true he came and took Papa away,' he continued.

Tanya still didn't answer.

Shura also broke off an icicle and put it in his mouth. The cold made his teeth hurt.

They both sucked on their icicles. From their expressions, it looked like it was the most important thing on earth. Both were deep in thought.

Shura stared at Tanya, his face deadly serious.

Tanya stared at Shura, her face equally serious. Then Tanya burst out giggling again, water spurting out of her mouth.

'You idiot,' said Shura, angry with his sister.

He waited until she stopped laughing.

'Think about it. Policemen don't just start chasing you for no reason!'

'Shura, he was just cross with us for talking a load of rubbish. For wasting his time. And plus, he must have realized we were bunking off school.'

Shura didn't know how to reply to that. They were both silent for a moment. Maybe his sister was right? He didn't know what to think.

'Hmm, OK,' said Shura, sliding off the bollard. 'Shall we go to The Nord, then?' He brushed the snow from the back of his coat.

'I know,' said Tanya. She chewed the rest of the icicle with a loud crunch, then explained. 'The Black Raven is a *raven*, and that's a big crow, right? And since crows and ravens are birds, let's go and ask the birds about him!'

Shura stared at her closely. Her face looked serious, but there was a mischievous glint in her eyes. Shura realized his sister was only trying to make him look silly by persuading him to talk to a bird. *But if I play along*, he reasoned, *then I can get her to do the talking, and she'll be the one who looks silly!*

'Yeah, good idea, Tanya,' he said, pretending to believe her. 'You go and ask.'

'You should ask,' Tanya insisted. 'You're the one who heard about the Black Raven.'

Shura knew his big sister was just trying to set things up so she could laugh at him, but he was determined to play the same trick on her. 'No, honestly, Tanya, I'd just ruin it again. Best that you do the talking!'

'No, really, you do it. Just ask them politely. Politeness works wonders.'

At that instant, with a rustle of their wings, two hooded crows landed in the public gardens nearby.

'Perfect!' exclaimed Tanya. 'Look, there're some crows right there!'

The birds, elegantly dressed in their dark-grey frock-coats, looked like they were holding their hands behind their backs, as they paced up and down in the slushy snow, carefully watching the ground for any movement.

'Oh, OK then,' Shura finally relented.

He saw Tanya's face light up triumphantly for a moment before quickly switching back to her feigned worried expression.

Just you wait, Tanya, he thought. *We'll see who's the winner this time.*

Shura started walking towards the crows. He slowed down, hesitated, pretending to his sister that he was feeling shy.

'What? What are you waiting for?' Tanya asked impatiently.

Now I've got you! Shura thought, confident that he could get her to speak to the crows instead of him.

'What should I say?' he asked.

'You know, just say what you heard. About the Raven and Papa.'

'No, I mean, *how* should I say it?'

Tanya rolled her eyes like she always did. 'Are you serious?'

Shura sighed, still acting. *Who's going to have the last laugh now, Tanya?* he thought to himself.

'Like this,' said Tanya. She stood up straight, her chest out and her hands held grandly in front of her as though she were about to make a speech.

The crows stopped and eyed her suspiciously.

'Most esteemed Comrade Crows, if you would please excuse us for bothering you, we would be grateful if you would kindly and graciously allow us to ask a question.' Tanya declaimed, all in one breath, carefully pausing where appropriate and enunciating clearly.

The crows glanced at one another, their dark grey eyelids blinking, the sunlight glinting dimly on their beaks.

'Got it?' Tanya turned to Shura.

And just as he was about to shout 'Ha! Tricked you!' and shove Tanya in the back, one of the crows opened his beak and said, 'Yes? Can I help you?'

The crow had a faint and slightly scratchy voice. The 'h' sounded more like 'kh'.

Shura's eyes opened wide in disbelief.

'Tanya, that was you . . .'

But Tanya stood there frozen, her mouth gaping. She was obviously struggling to breathe, but she tried to pull herself together.

The birds looked at them with a smug look.

'Go ahead,' the second crow added.

'Uh . . . uh . . .' Tanya mumbled.

'What's the time?' Shura blurted out suddenly.

'About ten o'clock in the morning,' came the crow's hoarse reply.

'Thank you very much,' replied Tanya, with a gulp.

The crows turned and began stalking away.

'What did you say that for?' Tanya hissed at Shura. 'You idiot!'

'You're the idiot!'

'You messed it up!'

'It was you who messed it up!' Shura rushed off after the crows. 'Comrade Crows! Comrade Crows!' *Address them politely*, he reminded himself. His heart was thumping. Thoughts galloped about in his mind in every direction at once.

The crows stopped and gave him a sidelong glance.

Tanya caught up with her brother. Sensing she was backing him up now, Shura spoke decisively. 'Comrade Crows! I won't keep you long,' he declared, while in his head he was thinking, *Huh? What's going on? What do I say now?* But it was too late to retreat. 'You see, our papa was taken by the Black Raven. And we're trying to find him. Do you know where we should look?'

The crows exchanged another glance.

'Yes, we know,' replied the second crow.

Shura buried his face in his sister's coat, stunned and afraid. Tanya put her arm around her brother.

'Would you be so kind as to tell us where he is?' she asked.

'No. We will not,' came the first crow's curt reply.

'Er . . . why not?'

'Because your intellect is considerably inferior to ours,' the crow willingly explained. 'You are of little interest to us. We interact only with our own kind. Come, my dear, let's be off.'

And with that the two crows strutted away arrogantly, with an occasional hop or a pause to peck at something in the wet snow. The children stared after them, stunned.

'Oh . . . that was a bit mean,' Shura said finally, his lips trembling.

'Ignore them,' whispered Tanya. 'There was no need for them to be rude.' She cleared her throat and patted her fist against her chest. 'Never mind, Shura,' she added in an almost normal voice. 'There are plenty of birds in Leningrad. Even in winter. They can't all be as big-headed as them. Maybe we'll meet the ones who come to our windowsill. I'm sure they'd help us. Even if we have to ask every single bird in Leningrad, that's what we'll do, Shura! We'll find this Black Raven! And we'll get Papa back. Today! We're not going to be bossed around by these feathery upstarts! . . . Come on!'

CHAPTER FIVE

Tanya and Shura walked out of the bakery on the corner of Nevsky Prospekt and Karavannaya Street with renewed determination. Tanya had a loaf of rye bread in her hand and Shura had a round white loaf.

The morning traffic had subsided. The wet pavements sparkled. The sun was peeping through the clouds: damp clouds with ragged edges that puffed along on the wind. The only people in the street were housewives out shopping.

'Let's go to the park in front of the theatre,' suggested Tanya. 'There are always lots of birds there.'

Shura shook his head. He was afraid he might bump into the spy in the hat again.

'All right,' Tanya quickly conceded. She had her own reasons for reconsidering. Those gardens were very busy with people meeting to play chess and others walking through: actors off to the theatre, students on their way to the library. If she and Shura were going to talk to the birds, the last thing they wanted was people overhearing.

'What about the park by the Engineers' Castle?' suggested Tanya.

Shura loved the pinkish-red castle with its green spire. It

had been built over a hundred years ago and was surrounded by a shallow moat with a real drawbridge. But there were no longer any knights anywhere to be seen. In fact, it wasn't much like the pictures of castles in Walter Scott's novels. But, even so, the very word 'castle' made his heart race. Shura imagined the tsar must have been a dreamer to have built a palace like this in the heart of his capital city.

So, they set off for the Engineers' Castle. For some reason there was never anyone there. And the gardens were deserted this time, too. The silhouettes of bare branches stood out against the bright-blue spring sky. There were no benches in this park, and therefore no old women, no nannies with hordes of children, no chess players and no dreamy lovers. There was nobody on the footpaths, either. People rarely crossed this park on their way to anywhere: they walked round it down Sadovaya Street, only their heads and shoulders visible from the park as they flashed past the cast-iron railings. The ambitious tsar who'd built this place lived here for just one month before he was assassinated, and rumour had it that his ghost could still be seen in the windows at night. Perhaps that was why people avoided the palace grounds. The only human form in the entire park was a huge statue of another tsar, Peter I, on horseback.

Tanya and Shura had a look around to make sure they found the best spot. They began to tear off pieces of bread and scatter the crumbs on the ground. Birds appeared out of nowhere, swooping in to hustle and push their way to the crumbs. The commotion rose as more joined the fray.

'Comrade Sparrows! Comrade Sparrows!' Shura tried to compete with their noise, to no avail.

'If you want any more,' shouted Tanya, raising the bread over her head, 'then first you need to answer our questions.'

None of the birds paid her the slightest attention. The surprisingly large flock of sparrows hopped about on their spindly legs. They bobbed up and down tirelessly like they were on springs. The bravest ones darted about between the children's boots, pecking at the crumbs. And they were all making a frightful din. The noise rang in the children's ears like the school bell at break-time.

'Would you please be quiet!' shouted Shura. 'I can't believe such little things can make so much noise!'

The sparrows stopped. Then they all started to chatter at once. 'Incredible! Did you hear that? The insolence! Calling us "little things"! Does he think we're children? We're adults with our own children to feed! Like we don't have enough on our plate without having to listen to such cheek! Never a second of rest! Foraging for food the whole day long! As if we had time to sit and chat with the likes of you! Well, I never!'

'Please!' said Tanya, remembering the magical power of politeness.

It was too late. With a *fr-rr-rr-rr*, the entire sparrow flock fluttered up into the branches, as if the bough had drawn them up with one inhaled breath. The small brown sparrows were completely invisible through the branches and dried leaves from last year. The bough seemed to be chirping and tweeting away by itself. All that could be heard was an agitated chatter:

'No! He said *what*?'

'Well, then he said . . .'

'You're kidding!'

'And I told him . . .'

'And what did he say?'

Tanya moved closer to the tree. 'Comrade Sparrows!'

The response was nothing but outraged chatter. All they could make out was the word 'impudence'.

'The pea-brains!' said Tanya, exasperated.

And at that the whole flock took flight and were off.

'Honestly, I would never get upset over a tiny thing like that!' insisted Shura. 'How silly!'

'I don't know if I should just feel glad that the birds are talking to us, at least. But I always thought sparrows seemed so sweet,' Tanya added thoughtfully.

'Well, never mind. I suppose they're just busy,' Shura replied. 'Oh, look, there's a magpie!'

The black-and-white magpie was bobbing up and down as it strutted about by the statue of Peter the Great. Against the background of the muddy soil and the slushy grey snow, the magpie seemed especially elegant, as if its white parts were washed and starched, and its black parts were smoothed down with a clothes brush. Its long tail and wing feathers were shot with splashes of green and blue.

As Shura and Tanya got closer, the shadow of the tsar's horse fell over them. The ground in the shade was moist and cold.

'What a beauty!' Tanya couldn't help but admire the magpie.

The magpie stopped, her tail quivering anxiously.

'First, let's throw her some crumbs. Show her that we come in peace,' Shura suggested.

'Better the white loaf than the rye,' said Tanya.

Shura threw a handful of crumbs, scattering them across the ground. But the magpie drew her head in between her shoulders and darted into the bushes, as if it were not crumbs that had fallen around her but bullets.

'Comrade Magpie!'

'Forgive us, please, for disturbing you!' Tanya said, addressing the bushes.

'Here's some lovely warm bread for you,' said Shura. 'Freshly baked today,' he added, carefully scattering the crumbs in a line, making a path from the bushes.

'I cannot bear to be caught off guard like that! You gave me quite a shock! Goodness me, you've set my heart into palpitations!' came a slightly crackled voice from within the bushes.

'Let's move away a little,' Tanya urged her brother. 'She's scared.'

They resumed negotiations from a respectful distance. 'Comrade Magpie, would you allow me to ask you a question?'

'A question? What question? Why are you asking questions? Goodness me, what impertinence! I'll have a heart attack with all your questions!'

'I'm sorry, but is it palpitations or a heart attack?' Tanya could not help being pedantic.

Shura punched her, softly. 'Our papa has been taken . . .'

This just made matters worse.

'It wasn't me! I haven't taken anything!' the magpie rattled off manically. 'It has nothing to do with me! I don't know anything! Haven't heard anything! Haven't seen anything!'

'We know that you didn't take him,' Tanya said, irritated now but trying not to show it. *What an air-head*, she mouthed silently.

'Our papa was taken by the Black Raven!' Shura hurried to clarify.

'No no no no no!' screeched the magpie. 'Don't tell me. I don't want to know. The less you know, the better you sleep. I keep myself to myself. I don't go poking my beak into other people's nests.' And, flashing greenish-blue in the sun, she fluttered away.

The magpie landed on the tsar's head, crowned with a laurel wreath. The reddish-tinged Engineers' Castle towered behind. The emperor didn't so much as twitch his eyebrows, but kept the same puffed-up, grim expression. With his formidable stare and a magpie on his head, he looked rather funny.

'What a self-centred coward!' shouted Tanya.

From beneath her tail, the magpie released a droplet, which glistened in the sunlight. It dripped on to the emperor's chest with a white splat.

'I know,' said Shura, emphasizing the vowel. 'And a scaredy-cat! I promise I won't ever be like that.'

'Shameful behaviour!' Tanya agreed. Then, looking at her brother, she exclaimed, 'Oi, Shura! What are you doing?'

Shura froze, a guilty look on his face. He had quietly

gnawed a hole in the white loaf. His cheeks were doing that telltale jolting from side to side. He looked at his sister, shamefaced, but he didn't stop chewing.

'Well, give me some, too.' Tanya grabbed the loaf and broke herself off a piece. Munching their bread, they left the park through the gates on to Sadovaya Street. Pedestrians scurried this way and that. Trams rattled past.

'Tanya, what other birds are there in winter?' asked Shura.

'Look!' his sister suddenly exclaimed. 'Look!' A parade of older children – Pioneers in their uniforms – was turning into Sadovaya Street from Field of Mars park.

Red calico banners, stretched out between two poles, drifted above the heads of the marching children, filling with air like sails. Alongside the banners floated an armada of plywood placards emblazoned with numbers. The zeros looked like astonished eyes or mouths wide open, aghast. The signs they held up proclaimed chilling statistics that sang the praises of various predatory birds. Tanya read them aloud for her brother.

'*The blue tit destroys six and a half million caterpillars per year*.

'And other insects,' Tanya added.

'*The goldcrest annihilates one million vermin per year*.'

Every board was crammed full of emotive words like 'destroy', 'exterminate', 'pests' and 'enemies'. Insect-eating birds were being celebrated for uniting against the trouble-makers, working together to clear them out of Soviet Leningrad once and for all. Some of the Pioneers carried little wooden birdhouses on poles, each with a round entrance hole and a little perch on the front.

'Ah, it's the Young Naturalists!' Tanya was delighted. 'They're sure to know.'

The changeable spring sunshine played on the copper trumpets the musicians carried. 'THANK YOU FOR OUR HAPPY CHILDHOOD!' proclaimed one banner that was radiant in the sunlight. The Pioneers' neckties fluttered like scarlet petals in the breeze.

'Hip hip hooray for Starling Day!' came the Pioneers' amicable and disorderly chant as they passed pedestrians, some of whom smiled while others quickened their pace with a scowl.

Tanya and Shura ran across the road and joined the tail end of the march, although they weren't yet old enough to join the Pioneers yet. The Pioneers turned to them with welcoming smiles.

'Hurrah!' shouted Shura. He stomped on the pavement with all his might, pumping his fists in the air.

'Excuse me, but where are the starlings?' asked Tanya, tapping someone on their grey-uniformed shoulder.

'What, you want us to find you some starlings?' The Pioneer laughed. 'This one's sweet!' he added patronizingly.

'What's so funny?' said Tanya, surprised.

'And let's . . . SING!' roared the parade leader.

The trumpets rose in the air and there was a rumble as the players blasted out the opening bars. The leader marched ahead of the column, waving her red flag like a conductor's baton. On her command, the Pioneers called out their chant, stretching words to the beat, so it almost passed for singing:

> *'Rejoice! Rejoice!*
> *The starlings are here*
> *And they're bringing good cheer.*
> *On their wings, in flies spring – come and see!'*

Shura couldn't resist joining in the rousing melody. He didn't know the words, but he opened his mouth and shouted 'A-ah-ah-ee!' in time with everyone else's vowels. Tanya ran to catch up with a tall girl, the leader, who was vigorously stamping her feet on the cobblestones.

'Excuse me, please.'

'What is it?' asked the leader, turning to her with a smile.

'Where are the starlings?'

The leader laughed loudly. 'They're coming!' And on she marched at the head of the column.

'The starlings fly back in April,' explained a chubby, serious-looking Pioneer in spectacles and a cap. 'But first we have to make birdhouses for them.'

'That's true,' Tanya agreed. But she couldn't help feeling a little disappointed.

'In the meantime we sing!' the ginger-haired boy in a cap beside him announced cheerfully. 'Can you sing?' he asked Tanya.

'I don't know,' Tanya replied.

'Of course she can!' shouted Shura. 'Who can't?'

Tanya shook her head and started trying to keep up with

the singers. Their chaotic yet cheerful song fluttered in the damp air, even drowning out the noise of the traffic.

> '*The starlings are hurrying homeward,*
> *Returning from warm climes to rest;*
> *Splish-splashing in streams and chit-chatting in trees,*
> *While they build their nests.*
> *And the soft breath of April's warm breeze blows*
> *Through grass, through the meadows and trees . . .*'

Drumming and tooting their trumpets, the Pioneers turned on to Nevsky Prospekt. When they reached the gardens surrounding the Pioneers' Palace, they lowered their banners and headed in through the gates.

'Stop!' Someone grabbed Shura and Tanya by the shoulders. 'You're not permitted to enter.'

The musicians lowered their trumpets. Like a large, bumpy caterpillar, the column of Pioneers slowly climbed the marble steps of the palace and were drawn in through the tall oak doors. But the grey-uniformed guard blocked Shura and Tanya's way and shoved them back on to the street.

'Why aren't we allowed in? We are Soviet children!'

'You're not Pioneers,' the guard said sternly.

'We will be soon,' Tanya retorted. 'I'm almost ten.'

'When you're old enough, you can join.'

'You're a representative of the obsolete generation,' Shura piped up, copying something he'd heard. 'You were raised under tsarism!'

'You little ruffian!' the guard gasped. 'Why aren't you at school?'

'Come back when you're old enough!' the leader of the march called down from the steps. She laughed, flashing her beautiful white teeth.

The guard rattled the gates.

'It's despicable that we still have guards like that in our Soviet nation!' fumed Tanya.

'We should report him to whoever's in charge,' Shura threatened. 'How dare he scare off future Pioneers!'

'Ah, forget it,' Tanya said, shrugging. 'Especially as the starlings haven't even arrived yet.'

'What now? Wait for April?'

'No, I've got an idea. Come on – let's go. Just round the corner.'

They dashed across Nevsky Prospekt, on to the bridge over the River Fontanka, narrowly avoiding a bus, whose driver angrily sounded the horn. On each corner of the wide Anichkov Bridge pranced four green-tinged bronze horses with flowing manes, each with a greenish-bronze athlete at their feet, leaning back and pulling their reins, struggling to control the wilful horses. The heads of the people walking past barely reached the top of the enormous stone pedestals on which these grand statues reared up.

Tanya ran to the railings between granite posts that stretched along the whole embankment and leant over to look down at the water. In summer, the river was full of ducks furiously paddling this way and that with their orange webbed feet. But now the water, black with cold, was empty of life and fringed at the edges with grey ice.

'Hmm. No ducks.'

Shura also looked down. The deserted water resembled a jet-black pupil surrounded by an ice-grey iris. Shura felt a sharp chill run through him at the lonely sight of the barren, icy river.

'Tanya, I know a bird that doesn't fly away in winter!'

'Which?'

'The swan in the Summer Garden.'

But Tanya didn't smile. 'Swans also migrate. They fly to India.'

'Not this one.'

'How do you know?'

'Because they clip its wings in the autumn and give it a little house for the winter. We went there on a school trip and they told us. What d'you think?'

'Good idea!'

The road alongside the River Fontanka led straight to the Summer Garden, and it wasn't far. But, as was obvious from its name, the park hibernated over winter. From the embankment Tanya and Shura approached the grand entrance gate, with its cast-iron railings adorned with angry female faces. The park was empty and desolate but for the straight dark outlines of bare trees. Through them you could see right down the park to the River Neva on the other side, which gleamed white beyond the trees' silhouettes. The gate was locked with a rusty padlock.

'Hmm ... That's the swan idea scrapped,' said Tanya, touching the lock. It had clearly not been opened for a long time.

'We could climb through the railings.'

'Are you insane?'

'We can sneak through quickly – no one will notice,' said Shura.

'I'm not climbing through anything.' All the same, Tanya looked around furtively. There were only a few passers-by, and they mostly looked down at their feet as they shuffled along, not up at the glorious city surrounding them, which showed off its best side here on this river bank. Tanya held her hand up to the iron bars.

'It's a narrow gap.'

'The main thing is getting your head through,' said Shura.

'We'll have to take off our coats or we'll never fit,' Tanya said, starting to undo her tight buttons. 'Shura, if I get bronchitis, it's all your fault!'

'Just pretend you've been walking fast and you're feeling hot.'

'We're not doing anything wrong, anyway. All we're doing is going to have a word with the swan, and then we'll be straight back out.' Tanya walked along the pavement with her coat unbuttoned and then, as quick as a lizard, she slipped out of her sleeves and through the railings, pulling her coat behind her.

'Shura!' she cried. 'Watch out!'

'Children! Can you not read the sign? The park is closed!' Out of nowhere, a woman in a fur hat appeared, clutching a handbag. 'Why are not you at school?' she asked, grabbing Shura by the collar.

'Let me go!' shouted Shura, twisting to get away.

'Our dog ran into the park!' Tanya cried, and, for the sake of authenticity, she started calling their imaginary dog: 'Bobka! Bobka!'

'Our dog's run away!' added Shura, wheezing for extra effect.

'Your sister can go and look for the dog, but you're staying here,' the woman said sternly, standing there as if she had nothing better to do. 'And where are your parents? Why are you walking the streets alone? Well? Where's your mother?'

Shura couldn't bear it when his mama was referred to as 'mother'. Such a grey, cardboardy sort of word. Desperate to get away and join Tanya, Shura squirmed and kicked hard. He must have hit the woman because she gasped and loosened her grip with shock. Shura pulled away and slipped through the railings into the park.

'Hooligans!' she shouted after him as he ran off. 'Crippling passers-by! I'll call the police! It's the orphanage for you!' The woman shook her skirt and her bruised leg as she screamed at Shura.

Inside the park, it was lovely and quiet. The noise of the city faded away in the distance. The statues were sheltered from the weather under tall wooden boxes that had turned grey from the damp. The trees stood knee-deep in the snow, which was dense and compacted here, and wet. The pond was still, like a dark mirror. The swan house stood proudly in the middle of the pond, its reflection echoing every single detail in reverse. It looked uninhabited, like a summer house boarded up for the winter.

'Are you sure that they clip the swan's wings?' asked Tanya.

Shura tried scattering a few small chunks of bread, tossing them carefully on to the pond. Each caused a ripple, but nothing else happened. The pieces turned soggy as they bobbed on the surface.

Suddenly there was a rustle; a faint slapping sound. Tanya gasped. An elegant swan, as white as snow and sugar, slid gracefully across the water. A triangular ripple fanned out in its wake, swelling with every moment.

'Look!' Shura shouted, although both of them were already staring in wonder at the grandeur of this bird.

'Esteemed Mr Swan,' Tanya said respectfully, pressing her hands to her cheeks. 'Thank you for staying here and not flying away to warmer climes.'

With a dignified gait, the swan climbed out of the water and gulped down the crumbs that Tanya spread before him on the ground one by one, shaking his head as he did so. He was in no hurry.

'Tanya,' whispered Shura, pointing at the woman with the handbag on the other side of the railings. She had been joined by a middle-aged policeman with a moustache, who was receiving a torrent of complaints from her. A bad sign. They needed to act without delay.

'Esteemed Mr Swan, the Black Raven has taken our papa away and we're looking for him,' said Tanya.

'The Black Raven himself finds those he requires,' pronounced the swan enigmatically.

'What do you mean?'

'Better, my dear, to answer another question: am I not the most handsome creature in this park?'

'Without a doubt you are!' Tanya was quick to respond. 'Do you know where the Black Raven is?'

'Naturally I do. I know everything. I am the most intelligent, too. But first, pray tell me: have you ever seen such a white neck?'

'Never. Your neck is the whitest in all of Leningrad.'

'Tanya, we need to hurry!'

'Am I not a more brilliant white than all these statues? They are but stone, after all,' continued the swan, studying his reflection in the dark water.

'You are the whitest of them all!' His sister was being such a suck-up.

'Tanya, enough. Can we get on with it?' groaned Shura. The policeman was clearly looking in their direction.

'Mr Swan, please tell us, where has the Raven taken our papa? Quickly, please!' Tanya begged.

Shura was jumping on the spot: they needed to run. There, on the other side of the railings, things were taking a nasty turn. The park-keeper had now joined the policeman and the woman with the handbag, and a bunch of keys rattled in his hand.

'My dear girl, remember, nothing is as harmful to beauty as needless hurrying,' the swan said in a didactic tone, tilting his head to one side as he admired his reflection in profile.

'Tanya, come on – he's wasting our time. He doesn't know anything.'

'I shall tell you what I know,' hissed the swan, but he was distracted again by his own reflection. 'A beautiful profile, is not it? A true, classical beauty.'

'Just answer my question, you stupid bird!' screamed Tanya. 'Or I'll tie a knot in your neck!'

'Tanya! They're coming!'

At that moment the park-keeper, the moustached policeman and the lady with the handbag burst through the unlocked gate and began heading towards the children along the main tree-lined path. The lady with the handbag pointed at Tanya and Shura, as if her finger could physically pin down the violators of public order.

Shura's heart was pounding. Tanya turned pale. There were now three people after them. The very mention of the Raven seemed to make people chase them.

On the right, the park was bordered by a small stream. To the left was the River Fontanka. Behind them were high railings topped with spikes. And ahead . . .

Tanya grabbed Shura's hand and rushed to the right. Behind them came an ear-piercing whistle. Then another.

While the policeman was taking a breath, the park-keeper blew his whistle. When the park-keeper took a breath, the policeman let out a trill. It made for quite a funny tune, in fact.

Their pursuers were lumbering along at a steady pace. Snow had started falling. Tanya and Shura slipped and tumbled down the gentle bank of the stream.

'Tanya, we'll get soaked!'

His sister squeezed his hand so hard it hurt. They landed on the ice – but nothing happened. The water was so shallow that it froze right through in winter, and although it was now spring the ice was still thick enough to hold their weight. Slipping and sliding, they ran to the other side; an ominous cracking sound came from the ice underfoot. Clawing at the bank on the other side, they clambered up the slope, where blades of grass poked out through the snow.

Behind them they heard a terrible crunch and then a squeal. Tanya and Shura turned round to see the park-keeper and policeman dragging the handbag lady out of the ditch. Her hat fell off on to the ice. Her handbag and the hem of her dress were drenched; the thawing ice couldn't hold her weight, it seemed. Her legs slid helplessly back down the slippery, snowy slope, as if she were running on the spot.

Tanya and Shura rushed headlong past the Field of Mars, past another sleepy park on the other side of the stream, and back towards the residential streets, where they could shake off their pursuers in the network of alleys and courtyards. They ran flat out, heading for the district where the turquoise and red cupolas of the old cathedral sparkled in the sky like decorated gingerbread. Very occasionally a passer-by would look at them askance. It was considered unseemly to run in the streets of this city with its stern, elegant houses, and its handsome squares, bridges and boulevards.

The children ran round the cathedral, across the bridge over the canal, and into a small, gloomy courtyard. The walls of the houses formed a cube around them with a square of sky straight above. Here they could pause and catch their breath. On the ground lay a pile of firewood, which had apparently just been delivered. It gave off a pleasant smell of resin. Shura sat down on the stack of wood. Tanya was inhaling deeply, trying to get her breath back.

'That's it,' Shura whimpered. 'I've had enough. I'm tired. I want to go home. I'm hungry, I'm thirsty and I need the toilet.'

'Shura, what's up with you?'

The sky gradually turned a deeper blue as the air grew cooler; the day was slowly giving way to evening.

'The police are after us, the birds are talking to us – I've had enough of this. I'm tired and I want to go home now. Come on, Tanya – let's go!'

'What about Papa?' asked Tanya, surprised that he had changed his tune.

'Mama said he's gone away for work! On a business trip. You said so yourself . . . Can we go home now? It must be nearly supper-time, and Mama and Bobka will be wondering where we are.'

Tanya sighed. 'Why don't we go to the movies on the way home, though? Seems silly not to. Mama gave us some money to have fun. All we've bought is *pirozhki*. And bread.'

'I don't want to go to the movies. I want to go home!'

'All right, no need to howl,' said Tanya, getting cross. 'You're the one who started with this Black Raven thing, by the way.'

'And now I've had enough!'

'OK. Come on, then.'

'Home?'

'Home.'

Shura sniffed, slid off the woodpile and brushed down his

coat. They walked out through the arch and along the canal towards Nevsky.

They decided they would stop at The Nord cafe and bakery as it was on their way home, after all. They had hot chocolate with whipped cream, and to take away with them they bought some lemonade and a box of little cakes and *petits fours*. The box was tied up with a silk ribbon. The glass bottles gently clinked in the paper bag.

A pigeon fluttered out from under their feet as they stepped out of the bakery. Presumably it would also be able to speak. But Shura was no longer in the mood to check. He imagined how they would sit with Mama, with a nice hot cup of tea and these tiny cupcakes and pastries, and his mouth watered. Tanya seemed to be thinking the same thing. Neither said a word the whole way home.

At the junction with Liteiny Prospekt, they crossed the road, cautiously hiding in the crowd of pedestrians from any policemen who might have been keeping an eye out for them. The woman who sold the hot, greasy pasties on the corner had apparently sold out, as she was now nowhere to be seen.

Tanya and Shura turned off the street towards their front door. The sky was now dark blue, as if infused with ink. A cosy, warm light seeped out of other people's windows, giving a gentle nudge to those who were not yet home.

The final walk up the stairs was a struggle; exhaustion made it seem as if the box was full not of cakes but rocks. At last there was the door to their communal flat, covered in nameplates for all of the families that lived there. Beside each name was an instruction on how to summon them. For Tanya and Shura's family, the instruction was: THREE LONG RINGS. But they didn't need to ring the bell; Tanya opened the door with her key.

In the dark shared corridor, a dim yellow light bulb flickered amid the usual sounds and smells. The murmur of a radio, a gramophone playing, a conversation among neighbours; someone was singing, others were arguing. The flat smelt of ten different dinners, all being prepared at the same time in the communal kitchen. It smelt of hot soapsuds; someone was boiling their laundry. It smelt of the old things forever exiled to the communal corridor from all the rooms where there was no space: bicycles, sledges, chests, washtubs. Shura and Tanya had long learnt to pass by without bumping into them, even in the dark. Just one thing was different to usual.

They stopped in front of their door.

'What's that?' asked Shura.

There was a narrow white strip of paper on the door, with something carelessly scribbled on it in illegible purple ink. Shura touched the red sealing-wax stamp, hanging from two strings. The strip of paper and the strings connected the door with the doorpost, so you couldn't open the door without tearing the strip and breaking the seal.

'Don't touch it, Shura!' Tanya stopped her brother. 'We don't know what it is.'

'Mama, are you there?' Shura drummed on the door. He

listened. Nothing. 'Mama!' Increasingly anxious, he banged the door with his foot.

Nearby a door creaked. The old woman who wasn't friends with anyone popped her grey shaggy-haired head round the door. 'Get out of here! Get away, quick!' she whispered, with fear in her voice.

'Why? Where's Mama?' Tanya asked loudly.

'I gave you the purse. Just be grateful that they were confused by the second door.'

'Who? What are you talking about?' Tanya demanded.

'Go to your aunt,' said the old woman. 'Like I told you. I've done all I can. I've had enough trouble.'

The door slammed shut and the key turned three times as the old woman locked herself in.

Tanya was furious. 'What's she being like that for?' she demanded.

'Where's Mama?' whimpered Shura.

Tanya took a deep breath. 'Hmm. It's too late to go to Auntie Vera's. Where else can we go? Let's go up to the attic for a bit,' Tanya suggested, keen to comfort her little brother. 'That's the best thing to do. We'll wait up there for Mama.'

'I'm hungry. I'm really tired,' whinged Shura.

'She must have been held up at work.' Tanya pulled her brother along with her to the attic, taking the key on the way from the peg on the wall. The attic was also a shared space, like the kitchen, bathroom and toilet. The neighbours took the key whenever they wanted to go up and hang out their washing or bring it in when it was dry.

'Let's call her at work,' said Shura.

'She's got a different job now, remember? And we haven't got the new number.'

'And Bobka?' Their footsteps echoed loudly on the stairs, walls and ceiling, which still had bumpy patterned bits from the olden days.

'He's with Mama. Where else would he be?' Tanya muttered, out of breath. 'She will have picked him up from nursery after work. And they must have gone to visit someone on the way home.'

The children went up to the attic and unlocked the hatch. The sheets and pillowcases hung up to dry responded with a sigh. Tanya pulled Shura inside.

'It's dark,' he grumbled.

'But it's almost warm. And your eyes will soon get used to it. Sit down here, on this crate. This one can be a table. And this newspaper can be the tablecloth.' Tanya smoothed out the rustling sheet of abandoned newspaper. Headlines in huge letters shouted about spies and enemies and the triumphs of Soviet workers. Tanya placed the cake box on top of it. She untied the ribbons. The sight of the lovely, delicate cakes and pastries was a good distraction from everything.

'Mmm, I'd like a *bouche*,' said Shura.

'But we haven't washed our hands,' said Tanya.

Shura wiped his hands on his coat. He saw his sister's reproachful look and sighed. Tanya went to the window, opened it and picked up some snow from the windowsill for them both. Their fingers turned red and stung from the cold. But having clean hands felt reassuring. Shura ate a *bouche* cream puff and Tanya had a cream horn. Then Tanya had an éclair and Shura had a cupcake. They shared a bottle of lemonade, taking it in turn to have a swig.

'Tanya. Hey, Tanya . . .' Shura began. But Tanya suddenly flung herself forward and banged on the crate. At the same instant, there was a flurry of wings beating noisily, throwing up dust. It was the pigeons that lived in the attic.

'Get out!' Tanya screamed, waving her hands in the air.

The pigeons settled back down on the floor like a quivering grey bedspread. A discontented hum spread among them, a nasal caw.

'Have you ever heard such a thing? And sitting there eating. Eating! In our loft! Eating our food!'

'It's not yours!' Tanya shouted at them.

'It's our loft! Our loft!'

'OK, we won't trouble you. We'll just sit here and wait for Mama. Then we'll go.'

'Left alone! Left alone!' the pigeons murmured among themselves. They always seemed to be in agreement.

'We're not alone, actually,' Shura objected.

'We'll just sit here a bit, then we'll go,' Tanya explained.

'We know your kind. First it's just once up here, then it's every night. Who are you with? Who are you?'

They had to explain about the Black Raven to stop the pigeons' endless questions. Suddenly in Shura's heart there was a flicker of hope: perhaps these nosy pigeons might know something?

'Disgraceful! A scandal!' they gurgled. But it wasn't clear to what or to whom they were referring.

'So, do you know where the Black Raven is?'

'Oh! Oh! Oh!'

'Do you know or not?'

'Ooh! Ooh! Ooh!'

'What imbeciles,' fumed Tanya. 'Spiteful imbeciles.'

'If you give us information we'll give you some cake,' Shura butted in. To no avail. The pigeons flew up, noisily flapping their wings. It became suffocating as they thrashed about in the air.

'Give it back!' they cooed. 'It's our loft! We live here! It's all ours!' They swooped at Tanya and Shura, pecking and scratching. Tanya pulled someone's towel off the washing line and began to spin it round like a propeller. The pigeons shied away.

'It's our loft! Our loft!' they squawked from a safe distance. 'Ours! Ours! Ours!'

'We'll see about that!' Tanya picked up a piece of wood that was lying on the floor and threw it at the pigeons.

They fluttered even further away. Now the cooing could be heard just faintly in the darkness, but you couldn't make out the individual words.

Shura was fed up with it all. He wanted to go back to the world where sparrows twittered, crows cawed, magpies chattered and pigeons cooed. Where Mama, Papa and Bobka were all at home waiting for them.

Tanya hugged him tightly. They squeezed into a corner, their arms around each other. They gazed into the darkness, alert to any sudden hostile moves. But the pigeons had either roosted for the night, or were pretending to be asleep. The

94

dark loft was full of shadows, rustles and sighs, and a stray moonbeam that softly caressed everything in its path. The shadows flickered along the walls and ceilings, with slow, unthreatening movements. They seemed to pour into Shura's eyes, filling them up from the inside. And Shura's tears flowed and flowed and flowed . . .

The first thing Shura saw in the morning was an empty box smeared with cream. Stuck to the traces of cream were a few bluish-grey feathers.

'Ugh, the vermin!' Shura kicked the box. But the pigeons were nowhere to be seen; they had long since flown off to attend to their daily business of rummaging through rubbish. Tanya was asleep, covered with a towel pulled up to her chin, the toes of her boots sticking out at the bottom.

'Tanya,' said Shura, giving his sister a gentle shake. 'We're going to get an earful from Mama.'

'What?' Tanya stretched out her legs and groaned. 'Ah, I've got pins and needles . . . Oh my goodness! Have we been here all night?'

'Mama will be out of her mind. She'll have got the neighbours out looking. She'll have called the police. Probably the hospital, too.'

'Oh my! We have to go – quickly!'

To their great relief, there was no longer a mysterious piece of paper on the door with someone's signature, or a seal dangling across it on strings. Shura laughed with relief. Tanya put the key in the keyhole. It wouldn't go in. She and Shura stared at the key, as if hoping to find the answer in the indentations.

Suddenly their door opened by itself. From the inside. Their neighbour Auntie Rita stood in the doorway in her dressing gown. She had curlers in her hair.

'What do you want?' she spat out with a scowl.

'Mmm-mmm-mama . . .' Shura softly whimpered.

'Where's our mama?' asked Tanya, trying to see behind Auntie Rita.

Their parents' room looked like yesterday morning. Only the clothes hanging up were someone else's. On the chest of drawers were someone else's photographs. And on the bed, under someone else's red blanket, lay Uncle Kolya, Rita's husband.

'Where do you think she is?' Auntie Rita snarled. 'Girl, are you a fool or just playing the fool? Get out of here, or I'll call the police.'

'My violin,' said Tanya, her lips barely moving, her eyes fixed on the case propped up against the stove.

'There's nothing of yours here any more. We live here now. Everything is ours now.'

'Give it to her, will you?' Uncle Kolya said lazily from the bed. 'What are you going to do with a fiddle? They might need to busk for a kopeck or two now they're orphans.'

The door slammed shut against Tanya's nose. Shura stood frozen, blinking. Tanya was pinned to the spot, neither alive nor dead. They could not fathom what they had just heard.

The door opened again. Tanya's hands clasped the cool, smooth case. The door slammed again. This time it was final.

Shura was so frightened that he couldn't even cry, he just trembled. A huge heavy thought entered his mind, but couldn't find space to settle, no matter how it tossed and turned. Tanya hugged her violin case to her chest.

'Now beat it!' someone yelled from the other end of the corridor.

The neighbours are quarrelling in the kitchen again, thought Shura.

Auntie Katya came running out of the kitchen – skinny, but strong and sinewy. In her wet red hands she had a tea towel. Her face was distorted with rage, like she'd been arguing.

The damp tea towel slapped Shura across the face. Then it hit Tanya.

'A fine mess we'll have to get ourselves out of because of you lot! Now beat it!' Auntie Katya began to shove them towards the door with both hands. She smelt of soap. She shook Shura out like a rag. 'Leave us alone!' she shouted. 'We still live here!'

'We still live here, too!' Shura squeaked.

'What are you doing?' Tanya screamed in desperation.

'There's nothing for you here any more!' Auntie Rita appeared at the door again, apparently eager to have the last word. The rest of the neighbours began to peek round their doors into the corridor.

'Help! Let me go!' Tanya tried to wriggle free. But no one stepped forward to help them. Auntie Katya pushed Tanya and Shura along the corridor.

'That's right! Send them packing! The enemies are swarming. Time to destroy their nest!'

'Get them out of here!'

'We've already had quite enough trouble!'

'But we haven't done anything!' shouted Shura, scared and confused.

No one replied. All the children could hear was a chatter of 'No!', 'No!', 'No!' rattling down the corridor, as all the doors slammed shut.

'*Back to normal, as if nothing's happened . . .*'

'*Don't say a word. I don't want to know . . .*'

'*The less you know, the better you sleep . . .*'

'*I don't know anything about it . . .*'

'*Didn't hear a thing . . . Didn't see a thing . . .*'

'*I always keep myself to myself . . .*'

The entire corridor had suddenly turned mute and blind.

Auntie Katya shoved the children out on to the landing, slamming the huge oak door shut in their faces. As the door swung towards them, the dim light glinted on the metal nameplates like a farewell wave. The lock clicked. The silence on the landing rang in their ears. Shura and Tanya were utterly alone.

'Look, Shura,' Tanya whispered, so softly he could barely hear.

Where yesterday there had been a metal nameplate with their name on and the instruction of THREE LONG RINGS, now all that remained were four holes from the screws.

There was something about those screw holes so final, so irrevocable, that it was too late to object.

'Come on. We'd better go to Auntie Vera's,' Tanya said in a colourless voice, touching Shura's shoulder.

He stared wide-eyed at the door; he knew for sure that something important had escaped through those four holes.

'Come on,' Tanya repeated. 'We have to get out of here.'

CHAPTER SIX

Outside in the yard, Shura was so stunned that he didn't cry. He just looked at his sister.

Tanya didn't cry either. A strange, crooked smile appeared on her face. Shura wondered if she was thinking what he was thinking. That Auntie Rita would run out of the front door after them — as she was, in her curlers and dressing gown — and shout, '*Only kidding! Didn't you realize it was a joke?*' And their mama would follow, laughing. '*Tanya, Shura, I was hiding under the stairs! I was being silly. Sorry. Forgive me?*' And Bobka would toddle about, getting under everyone's feet. And then Papa would come home.

A man came out from the next archway. It was the caretaker, wearing a big thick hat. His bushy eyebrows and beard, the badge on his apron, and his whistle — which he would blow to instantly summon a police officer out of nowhere — all inspired nervous giggles among the boys in the street.

The caretaker began to sweep aside the melting snow with a bristly birch-twig broom, leaving tracks with each movement.

'Tanya, we could complain to the caretaker?'

Everyone was afraid of him, including the neighbour-hood's stray dogs, pigeons, cats and drunkards, and even the quarrelsome neighbours.

If you don't work hard, you'll end up a caretaker – Papa's voice popped into Shura's head.

The caretaker didn't look at them. He looked down as he swept the slushy ground with his broom. 'How could your mother and father do such a thing?' he muttered into his beard. He turned to walk away.

'What did you say?' Tanya burst out. 'No, wait!' she shouted, rushing after him. She had the violin case in one hand, and dragged Shura along with the other. She blocked the man's path. 'What did you say?'

'They seemed like decent Soviet people. But they turned out to be spies. Enemies of the people. They let everybody down.' His voice sounded strangely artificial. Too loud. He was enunciating more clearly than usual, as though he were on stage. His eyes darted about.

'Who told you?' asked Tanya.

'No one needed to. The Raven took them – it's obvious,' the caretaker muttered, looking away.

'The Raven?' Shura repeated. He thought he must have misheard.

'Raven?' Tanya stopped. She almost burst into tears at this ill-timed joke. 'It's not funny!' She was angry now. 'Do you hear? It's not funny!'

'So they must have been guilty,' the man declared, in an unnaturally emphatic voice. His face wrinkled, as if from pain. He quickly turned away. 'Get away from here,' he whispered suddenly. 'Go to your aunt. Like you were told you to! You silly kids. Go quickly now, before it's too late.'

Behind him Tanya saw a curtain flicker in a window on the ground floor. A nose poking out. Why was the caretaker acting so strangely? What did he want from them?

'Get away from here! Or I'll call the police. Be off with you!' The caretaker put his whistle up to his mouth. But his eyes were not threatening; if anything, they were imploring Shura and Tanya to listen to him. He waved his broom at them. '*Kshhh! Kshhh!*' he hissed, like you would at a stray cat. 'Get away from here!'

Tanya and Shura jumped back.

'*Kshhh!*' He bashed his broom on the ground, sending snow flying in their direction.

Tanya and Shura turned and made a run for it. They were followed by a faint whistle, more for show than anything.

Tanya and Shura didn't see the curtain twitch and the nose disappear.

At first they ran. Then they slowed to a walking pace. They walked and walked. Every now and then someone bumped into them with a bag, a briefcase or an arm, and the jolt would make them change direction and they would wander on until another jolt sent them in another direction. To and fro they went, twice crossing the bridge with the greeny-bronze griffins sitting on the four corners with street lamps on stalks on their heads.

'Shura, we're going the wrong way,' said Tanya, as though she was coming round from a daze. Her voice was strange.

She didn't seem to really care that they had been going in completely the wrong direction.

'I know,' said Shura, as reluctant as his sister to start heading the right way.

Their aunt lived far away, over the river in the Petrogradskaya district of the city. They had to go by tram over the bridge. Neither of them wanted to go to hers. They couldn't! They both felt it. As if getting on a tram meant accepting that what the caretaker had said was true. As if going to their aunt meant being forever cut off from their normal life – the one where they had Papa, Mama and Bobka. And their home.

It seemed as though, while they wandered aimlessly around the city like this, it was still a game. It was still possible to go back. To win the game.

'I'm hungry. And thirsty.' Shura stretched his frozen fingers and clenched them into a fist. Ahead of them was the beautiful greyish-yellow cathedral with its green dome. Its semicircular colonnade curved outward like giant stone arms reaching to embrace the two bronze statues of generals looking out over Nevsky Prospekt.

Tanya put her violin case down on the pavement. She pulled out the purse from their mother and counted how much money they had left. They still had plenty. But they both instinctively knew that they needed to spend it wisely.

'Come on. We've got enough for breakfast.'

But Shura didn't move.

'What's wrong?'

'Tanya . . .'

'What?

'I need to pee.'

'Well, go in the bushes somewhere. Turn away from the street . . . and pee!'

Shura shook his head.

'I'll keep watch,' Tanya reassured him.

'I can't.'

Tanya rolled her eyes with a sigh. 'What do you want – a drink or a pee?' she quipped. But she took his hand. 'Come on.'

They went into a bakery. Shura listened to Tanya telling the saleswoman a fib about a music lesson. The saleswoman in the white cap nodded sceptically. Tanya raised her violin case above the counter. It worked: the saleswoman lifted the counter to let them through to the back.

'And why are you alone?' she asked. 'Without an adult?'

'Our grandmother is waiting for us at Gostiny Dvor,' Tanya lied.

While Shura was busy with his buttons and braces, Tanya saw how the saleswoman nodded to her colleague who wore the same white hat, then went over to the black shiny telephone and picked up the receiver.

'Shura, we need to run,' whispered Tanya. They tumbled back into the shop and dashed out on to the street, Shura fastening his buttons as he ran. Customers looked on, puzzled.

They darted into the first archway they came to.

'Tanya, what is this? Do we have to run away from everyone now?'

'How should I know?' Tanya snapped. She peered cautiously out into the street.

There was no one following them.

'The coast is clear,' she declared. But, instead of going out on to the street, she leant against the wall, her leg bent at the knee and her foot against the brickwork. 'The only thing that's clear right now is that the Raven is not made up.'

At any other time Shura would have shrieked with joy: 'I told you so!' But now he just looked at his sister in fright.

'I don't understand why she said "they",' said Tanya. 'The old woman. She said "they". And the caretaker said "the Raven".'

'I guess there were two of them. Two ravens.'

Tanya looked at her brother. 'You don't get it, do you?'

'What?'

'They would have taken us away, too.'

'Who?'

'We were lucky. They didn't realize that the wardrobe was the door to our room.'

Shura remembered: *That's right!* He did hear a knock on the main door from the corridor, but no one had checked the wardrobe door.

And they spent the second night in the attic. 'They' didn't know that. It? Or he? The Raven. Shura imagined a crow, but bigger. In their corridor. In their bedroom. The raven leans over Bobka's cot, lifts Bobka up by his pyjamas with his beak . . . *No, it can't be true! That can't happen!*

'Come on. We need to eat,' said Tanya, picking up the violin case and resolutely walking through the archway that led back to the street. Shura trailed after her.

★

They lost track of how many hours they wandered around the city, following the loops of the canals, the meandering alleys, the neat, straight lines of the streets. They had a bite to eat. Then they started walking again.

The day quickly burnt out. The sky took on an orange hue. It began to get dark.

Gradually Tanya's footsteps took on a certain purposefulness. Shura realized that they were on their way to Auntie Vera. They needed to get to the River Neva. They would see the golden spire of the Peter and Paul Fortress in the distance, and the blue domes of the mosque behind the dense, yet bare, trees. A bridge would lead them slowly in that direction, wide and long, like a broad avenue. Tanya seemed to be walking towards the Neva. Shura hoped that she knew the way.

They were afraid to get on a tram, under the scrutinizing gaze of the conductor.

'Hang on,' said Tanya, a look of realization on her face. 'What if she doesn't know that we're coming?'

'Who?'

'Auntie Vera. What if Mama hadn't called her?' Tanya muttered, talking more to herself than to Shura. 'What if Auntie Vera also turns against us? What if, when she opens the door, she takes one look at us and calls the police?'

Tanya slowed her pace. She stopped. Her legs ached. Her feet were frozen, tingling with each step like pins and needles.

The windows of the houses were starting to light up. Their warm glow seemed to mock them.

'Tanya, come on,' Shura called.

'And what if we have to spend the rest of our lives running away?' His sister bit her lips. She had shadows under her eyes. And a wrinkled forehead.

Shura didn't know the answer.

'And what if Mama and Papa really are . . . like that?'

'Like what?' Shura could not even utter the terrifying word.

'Like the caretaker said.' Tanya's eyes narrowed, her nostrils flared. 'Maybe there *is* something they haven't told us!'

They avoided looking each other in the eye. Instead, they rested their elbows on the granite parapet of the bridge and pretended they were examining the water. It looked purple.

'Come on,' said Tanya finally. 'It's cold. It's getting dark.'

They turned into a gloomy arched tunnel, walking alongside the River Moyka as it flowed through to join the Neva. Under the arch, the water splashed and gurgled, and patches of reflected light danced on the curved walls. They came out and suddenly before them was a great expanse of sky and water. The Neva drifted slowly away from the city.

'Look,' said Tanya. In the air hung a flock of seagulls spreading their wings wide. They seemed as though they were cut out of tin foil. The gulls allowed the wind to pull them to the side, then with a few flaps of their wings they returned to where they were before.

The breeze rummaged under Shura's coat. Tanya pulled her hat down tightly over her ears. The wind had plenty of room to gather momentum over the broad river.

Tanya had a determined look on her face.

'I don't want to talk to any more birds,' Shura was quick to stress.

At that moment along the entire length of the embankment, to the left and to the right, the street lamps suddenly lit up with their milky glow. It was dusk.

'We should go to Auntie Vera's now,' said Shura. 'Let's go quickly.'

'So, are you giving up?' Tanya's eyes narrowed again. 'Do you give up? Just say so, you miserable little coward.' She ran over to the granite wall that ran along the river. 'Comrade Seagulls! Comrade Seagulls!'

'Tanya, stop it! It's not funny!'

'I'm not laughing,' his sister snapped.

'Tanya!'

'Who else should we ask? When everyone else hurls themselves at us like we're criminals! Like thieves or worse . . . Comrade Seagulls!'

It looked to Shura as though the gulls were being blown closer to them by the wind. They just needed to tip their wings ever so slightly, it seemed, and the wind carried them to wherever they wanted.

'Tanya!'

'Fool,' Tanya growled, and again she shouted, 'Comrade Seagulls!'

One of them sank to the wall with a great clatter of its wings. Eyeing them suspiciously, the seagull smoothed a twisted feather back into place with its beak.

Tanya glanced triumphantly at Shura, as if to say, *Did you see that?*

'Comrade Seagull, we're all alone. What should we do now?'

The seagull shifted several times from foot to foot.

'Take a leaf out of our book.' Its voice was thin and piercing. 'We're on our own. We owe nothing to no one – and no one owes us anything. That's freedom!'

'If we listen to you –' Shura said.

'Shut up, you coward,' interrupted Tanya. She turned back to the seagull: 'It's getting late. We need to find our mama and papa somehow. And Bobka – that's our brother, he's little.'

'It is late,' the seagull creaked, tilting its head. It was either agreeing with Tanya, or disagreeing. A gust of wind ruffled its feathers. 'It is *late*,' the seagull repeated, stressing the word mysteriously. Did it mean that it was *too late*? Or just that the sun had set and night was descending on the city?

'May I ask you something?' Tanya looked wistfully at the seagull.

'Please do.'

'May I stroke you?'

The seagull, shuffling from one foot to the other, turned its side to face Tanya. She carefully reached out her hand. The seagull was surprisingly solid and smooth to the touch.

Shura lost patience with Tanya for her frivolous behaviour. The seagulls could see everything from above: it was time to come out and ask them straight.

'The Black Raven!' shouted Shura, emerging from behind Tanya to face the seagull. 'Have you heard about the Black Raven?'

The seagull noisily launched itself into the air and in the blink of an eye was soaring high. It blended into the flock where it could no longer be distinguished from the others.

'Raven! Raven! Raven! There! There! There!' they crowed, maybe crying, maybe laughing, as they swayed in the wind.

At that moment the rumble of an engine could be heard. It was coming from further down the embankment.

'Tanya, the Raven is here! Tanya! Run!' screamed Shura, making a dash towards the houses.

Tanya rushed headlong after him.

They dived through a front door on the embankment into the entrance hall of a house. A shaft of light from the street lamp outside passed through a murky window that hadn't been washed for a long time, revealing a colourful tiled floor in the hallway. In the twilight, they could see a marble Cupid with a broken wing. Once, under the tsar, this house must have been rich and luxurious. Now, like the building where Tanya and Shura lived, it was inhabited by new tenants who had never experienced luxury, who lived with one family in each room. Because in the Soviet Union everyone was equal.

'Who was it?' Tanya asked in a whisper, silently placing the violin case on the floor.

'I didn't see,' whispered Shura.

'But you shouted "Raven"!' Tanya clasped her hands in frustration.

'*They* shouted "Raven" . . . and I thought . . . Oh, Tanya! It's just that – I heard that seagulls have really good eyesight!'

'Oh, Shura . . .'

Tanya kicked the violin case in irritation. The violin moaned.

'Panicking me like that!' Tanya's voice rang in his ears. 'You scared the seagull off for nothing. Because of you, we got nothing from that conversation! You coward!'

'I'm a coward?'

'An idiotic coward! This whole mess is because of you and that spy with the ice cream! And now you won't do anything to help! You snivelly coward!' Tanya stamped her feet.

'I'm *not* a coward!' Shura tugged the handle of the door and leapt outside, slamming the door shut behind him. The rumbling engine sound was very close now.

'Hmph!' snorted Shura, enraged with his know-it-all sister.

'Shura, stop!'

But Shura wasn't going to listen to her any more. *I'll show her!* He grabbed a nearby stick from the ground and slotted it through the door-handles on the outside.

. . .

Later he would struggle to explain why he did what he did.

'Could it be, Tanya, that I understood something at that moment? Was that it . . . ?'

. . .

Tanya rattled the door from the inside, to no avail.

'Shura!' came her muffled cry. 'Open the door!'

'Tanya, don't shout,' Shura tried to speak calmly. 'One of the tenants will let you out. Don't be afraid! The main thing is – you go to Auntie Vera, I'm going to find the others!'

I'll show her. She thinks I'm a coward. Well, I'm going to find Mama, Bobka and Papa, and then we'll see what she says.

'Shura! For goodness' sake!' Tanya howled from inside the porch.

Shura pressed his back against the door, as if the gesture could settle her and stop her shoving. Tanya was beating against it with her shoulders. With each jolt, the pillars of light along the embankment seemed to bounce up and down.

'Shura, don't be stupid!'

The Raven himself will take me to them.

Shura rushed away from the house and his enraged sister, telling himself it was to save her from being caught. He ran along the pavement . . .

Towards the raven-black car that growled menacingly as it rumbled down the road.

The Black Raven crept slowly along the embankment, as if listening to the houses and windows. He seemed huge, but otherwise quite ordinary – the kind you see everywhere on the streets. This made him especially frightening, with his lacquered, black wings gleaming.

Shura ran to meet him, waving his arms. His heart was throbbing painfully in his chest. He was terrified.

I'm no coward, Shura told himself. *I'll prove it to her.*

'Hey! Hey, you . . . You're looking for me.'

The Raven stopped. Shura stood directly in front of him. He felt hot and clammy under his armpits. The Raven's crooked eyes peered at Shura without any expression.

And Shura said: 'I'm here.'

CHAPTER SEVEN

Shura didn't know where he was. He remembered running along the embankment towards the Black Raven and seeing the street lamps with their heads bowed down. He recalled being grabbed around the middle. Being somewhere dark that smelt of tobacco. Then somewhere dark and bumpy. Then dark again. And then – this woman in the headscarf. She had signed for him, then brought him here.

It appeared that the Raven loved the colour grey. Everything here was either grey or grey-tinged. One shade of grey or another. Sometimes the grey was combined with another colour. Just the slightest hint. But it seemed that was only when it couldn't be avoided, perhaps if they had run out of paint.

From the floor to halfway up, the walls were grey-green, and from the middle to the top grey-yellow. The floor tiles were grey-brown. There was a wire mesh cage over the ceiling bulbs, blocking some of the light. The walls and the dimness immediately made Shura feel drowsy.

'Sit up straight!' barked the woman from where she was sitting at a large table. She herself was grey. When he first saw her, standing up, Shura thought she looked like two grey squares, one on top of the other: a blouse-square on top of a skirt-square, and at the bottom two bollard-legs in grey stockings and grey felt shoes.

Shura straightened up in fright. For a moment he thought he recognized her: Auntie Dusya?

The woman bowed her grey-headscarfed head and went back to scribbling in her large notebook.

No – what made me think of Auntie Dusya? In his head, Shura gave the square grey woman the name Bollard.

There was one window in the room. It was half-painted over with grey-white paint. As if they didn't want anyone to look in and see . . . see what?

She scraped her chair back and stood up. She opened a drawer and took something out. She walked over to Shura. She wrapped a greyish-coloured sheet around him, up to his chin. Shura heard a clicking sound right by his ear. He felt something cold touch against his neck and head. He saw how his own hair began to fall down on to his lap. With a click-clacking handheld clipper, the woman was cutting tracks across Shura's scalp. Tufts of hair fell gently on to his knees and shoulders, or tumbled down the sheet on to the floor. His head felt cool, but in places it burned.

How is Tanya? How is she doing? Shura thought. *Please let them not have caught her.*

He wasn't scared. Shura felt like he had withdrawn within himself to hide, like a hare in its burrow.

'Take off your clothes,' boomed the enormous woman.

Shura struggled with his disobedient buttons. Why were his fingers trembling? After all, he wasn't afraid.

He neatly folded his clothes on top of his boots. He stood there naked, trembling. The floor under his feet felt ice cold.

The woman thrust a pile of grey clothes and boots into his hands. They looked like pyjamas. He put them on and then sat back down to pull on the boots.

'They're too big for me,' said Shura.

'I beg your pardon?' Bollard suddenly screamed. 'You say: *Thank you!*' She slammed both hands on the table.

Shura flinched.

'You filthy son of the enemy! We should be pulling your feet off, not giving you new boots! You be grateful.'

How dare she?

'I'm not an enemy! I'm a Soviet citizen!' Shura was surprised by how squeaky his voice sounded.

'Enemy. And a spy.' She pronounced it *shpy*. 'And your parents are enemies and spies.'

'Liar! That's not true!'

She gasped, shocked at his brazen response. Her mouth gaped open.

Shura slipped off the stool. He rushed to the door and yanked the handle. It was locked. He rushed about the room. He could smash a chair against the painted glass of the door – or the window?

Her little piggy eyes watched him without emotion.

Shura grabbed the stool. Suddenly he was deafened by a strong blow to the side of his head. Shura fell and clutched his ear. The shock was greater than the pain.

'What are you . . .?' Shura had been in fights before, and had been beaten up several times. But they were yard fights.

Boys messing around. And sometimes he got into a scrap with Tanya. His older sister was stronger and she'd always win. But being beaten by a grown-up?

'You're getting on my nerves,' said the woman calmly. She lifted Shura by the collar with one hand, turned the stool upright with the other, and flung Shura on to it.

'Sit straight, like I told you.' The woman pressed a metal button. A bell rang somewhere inside the building.

Shura's entire body trembled.

Where's Tanya? How is she?

'Your parents are spies. Spies and enemies. You say thank you. Here you will be made into a man. You will be re-educated.'

Shura was shaking all over.

He should never have run out of the porch like that! How did he think that he could cope alone? *Please let them not have caught Tanya*, he thought.

A neat man appeared, in greyish overalls with grey sleeve-covers. He hung a wooden sign around Shura's neck with a number written on it.

The goldcrest annihilates one million vermin a year – Shura suddenly remembered the Pioneers' placards. His hands felt like they had turned to ice. The man in the overalls set up a black tripod. The legs tapped on the hard floor. He secured a camera on top. He held up a grey plate on a handle.

'Look this way.' His voice was pleasant, soft. His eyes were blank.

No longer able to object, Shura stared straight ahead, where the man indicated. The plate flashed a dazzling light.

Shura blinked. The man took the board from around Shura's neck, folded up the tripod and left the room.

'Boots,' Bollard reminded him.

Shura thrust his feet into the boots.

Black spots with white edges still floated before his eyes from the flash. Bollard dragged him along the corridor by the collar. The long, narrow corridor seemed endless. On the high ceiling were the same lights encased in wire mesh.

The backs of the oversized boots slapped against his ankles. They almost fell off his feet.

Bollard pushed a tall heavy door with a strong freckled hand.

The light in the room was grey, like the light on a rainy day. A broad red carpet led from the door to a huge writing desk. On it stood a comforting tray of tea. Watching over the desk was a portrait of a man with a sizeable nose. Beneath the portrait stood a soldier. He gestured as if to say, *Come here*.

'Where are you going?' barked Bollard. 'Get back!'

Shura drew his head into his shoulders. Who should he listen to?

'How dare you trample the carpet with your hostile feet? Walk on the bare floor!' she yelled, jabbing Shura in the back. Obediently, he shuffled in his boots alongside the carpet.

The soldier opened a box, without uttering a word or looking at Shura, as if he were not standing there at all. Inside the box was a purple ink-pad.

Turning over Shura's hands, as if he were an inanimate object, the soldier pressed Shura's fingers firmly on to the pad, then pushed them on to a piece of paper one at a time.

Next, bowing his bald, shiny head, he began to write something. He did not even nod to Bollard.

She backed away obsequiously, dragging Shura out of the room.

The long corridor again. The dim lamps again. The grey walls again.

In another room Shura was given a scratchy grey blanket. In the next room he received a short grey coat and a grey cap.

The final room was a dormitory. The creaking of the door sent a barely perceptible tremor through the room. Everyone froze.

Shura could not believe his eyes. A row of identical metal beds lined the room from one wall to the other, all squeezed close together, made up with the same grey blankets. Near the beds, children stood to attention, their arms at their sides and looking straight ahead, each dressed in the same grey pyjamas. The woman shoved Shura towards a spare bed. The door slammed shut.

Again, a tremor rippled through the room, as everyone seemed to exhale. Some sat down. Some lay down. Someone walked over to a friend.

Two children cautiously inched their way over to Shura, marking out loops and circles on the ground. The two pale creatures with hedgehog bristles for hair considered the newcomer, silently and seriously. Shura pretended he hadn't noticed them. He spread out his blanket and tucked it in at the sides, like all the other beds.

'Are you a boy or a girl?' whispered one of the creatures staring at him.

Shura turned round. The whole room was listening.

'I'm a boy,' he said in a clear voice. He was ready to fight, if necessary.

The two creatures looked at his clenched fists. The second one – not the one who asked the question, or maybe it was? – laughed ever so quietly.

'Don't be afraid – we're just spies and enemies of the people here.'

Shura felt for a moment as though his heart had stopped.

'I'm not an enemy!' he yelled. 'I'm not a spy!'

'I'm Zoya, and this is Mitya,' said one of the creatures, who seemed not to have heard Shura's outburst.

'I'm not an enemy!' Shura shouted louder.

'What's your name? Your real name?'

Shura was surprised by the strange question. Why would he have a not-real name?

Suddenly a loud bell rang. There seemed to be a system of bells wired throughout the building, from the cellar all the way up to the attic. The grey children quickly formed into pairs, bumping into each other as they silently shuffled about. Zoya and Mitya, who still looked the same to Shura, nudged Shura in front of them. A boy with sticky-out ears came and stood next to him.

'I'm Anya,' said the 'boy' and added, 'That's my real name.'

'I'm Shura,' said Shura, addressing all three of them. Like them, he added that it was his 'real name', although he still had no idea what they meant by that.

Just let that Raven show up, Shura said to himself. *I'll ask him straight out. Let him give me an answer!*

They stomped along the corridor in a line following a gaunt, gloomy-looking woman in a grey uniform, like everybody here.

When they reached their destination, Bollard was standing at the doorway with a register in her hand. Checking the children against her list, she called out: 'Novembrina! Tractorina! Lenmarx!'

The children streamed inside in pairs. Bollard ticked them off her list. Inside, everyone sat down silently at the tables.

'Communisa! Vladilen! Mirrev! Octobrina!' To Shura's great surprise, Anya moved forward at the word 'Octobrina'.

'Stalchil!'

Shura remained standing, waiting for his name to be called.

'Stalchil!' barked Bollard.

'Go, go,' Zoya and Mitya whispered to him from behind, both sounding anxious.

Shura shrugged, unsure what to do. He certainly didn't want to get it wrong and annoy the bad-tempered Bollard.

But Bollard suddenly grabbed Shura by the ear. His eyes watered, and she yelled into his ear: 'Stalchil! Are you deaf?' shoving him over the threshold.

Shura could barely breathe as he walked into a room filled with steamy mist.

The walls in the hall were tiled, and the ceiling seemed low because of the white steam filling the air. The room was crammed full of tables and chairs. It smelt of food. This was the dining room.

A banner stretched right across the far wall proclaiming in large letters: WHEN I EAT, I AM DEAF AND MUTE.

Shura sat down next to Anya-Octobrina. His ear burned with pain. Mitya and Zoya took their places opposite them.

The roll call continued. The names flying about seemed to get stranger and stranger. They weren't regular people's names!

The children all flowed into the room and sat down.

'What's this about *Stalchil*?' asked Shura indignantly, but in a whisper, just in case.

'Stalin loves children. Stal-chil for short,' explained Anya-Octobrina.

'That's what you're called here from now on,' added Mitya.

Here.

'That doesn't make any sense! Stalin *is* a friend of the children,' said Shura, quoting what he'd heard his teacher say, 'but there's nothing friendly about this place!' Shura was fuming.

His new friends took no notice.

Mitya continued, 'I'm Vors, and she's Ninel.' He nodded at Zoya. 'That's Lenin backwards: Lenin – Ninel.'

'Wha-a-at?'

'You'd better remember and respond to your new name,' little Zoya added softly. 'Or you'll be in trouble.'

'Silence!' Bollard roared from the other end of the dining room.

Cooks in grey overalls and hats walked around the tables, hugging large grey pans that gushed out steam. They proceeded to slosh ladles of grey porridge into the children's bowls. Shura had a grey tin bowl and a tin spoon. The greyish sludge slopped into the bowl with a splat.

'Eat it up, enemy.'

Shura wanted to say, 'I'm not eating that.' But he saw a large freckled fist appear near his nose. He pushed some porridge on to his spoon.

'You be grateful that an enemy like you is getting fed.'

A glass of murky, greyish-brown tea landed on the table with a thump.

Shura gulped. There was no way he could swallow that unappetizing sludge.

'Do as she says, or it'll be worse,' Zoya whispered. 'Drink it.'

Shura waited anxiously for his stomach to lurch, sure that he was about to throw up every mouthful of the slimy gruel – on to the table, his knees, the floor – and that the terrifying woman would lay into him again. But he didn't. In fact, it settled warmly in his stomach.

'Where's your mother? And yours? Where are your parents?' he whispered to his new friends.

'We don't have parents.'

'You must have. Everyone has parents. Even flies.'

'No one here has parents.'

Shura wanted to protest. But there was something about having food in his tummy that made him suddenly lose his train of thought . . .

The grey days began to flow into an endless stream. After breakfast they were always taken to a large room with a glass ceiling where the light that filtered through was also grey. They sat down to work at rows of sewing machines.

Shura was quick to master the machine. There was nothing to it. You just lifted the foot, inserted two grey squares and stitched them together along three edges. The squares were piled up on the left. When the bags were finished you had to pile them up on the right. Bollard would pace up and down between the rows of bodies hunched over their work.

'Be grateful that we are teaching you a useful profession,' she reminded them. She tapped a long wooden ruler in the palm of her hand. If she noticed a wobbly line of stitches, Bollard would say with relish: 'Hold out your hands.'

The ruler rose in the air . . . and then *SLAM*! A burning agony spread through the outstretched fingers.

Everyone worked as hard as they could, including Shura.

The grey sackcloth crept along under the needle. The machines rattled along. The racket echoed off the bare walls.

On the first day Shura didn't think he would manage even an hour. At school, he always felt itchy and fidgety from having to sit still at a desk for hours on end. But here he quickly got used to it. Staring at the line of stitches as the needle jumped along, with the clatter of machines in the background, made his head muffled and cloudy.

The time flitted by somehow or other. The pile on the left gradually went down and the pile on the right grew. Then, before he knew it, it was dinner-time. In the foggy mist of the dining hall, the cooks served out some bland, greyish slop. Then the children were led out in pairs to stretch their legs in the yard.

Or the children were made to sit on very hard chairs while they had the newspapers read to them. The grey pages would rustle as Bollard – or the other warden, Big Nose – would shake the paper out to read it aloud, holding the print close to her face. The children looked at her obediently. Their hedgehog haircuts and their submissive, blank expressions made them indistinguishable. Had they in fact all become completely identical?

The voice droned on, intoning the same words: spies, saboteurs, enemies of the people, heroic feat, patriotism, motherland, our glorious leader. Today's newspaper was exactly the same as yesterday's, and the one the day before yesterday, and tomorrow.

Then it was supper.

The days clodded together into an indistinguishable greyish lump. Shura soon lost track of how long he had been there. A peaceful indifference washed over him. Shura no longer worried about where Tanya was, whether she had managed to escape from the porch, whether she had made it to their aunt's. What was their aunt called, anyway? He no longer knew. Lera? Era? He soon gave up trying to remember. Never mind, he'd think, brushing it off. And then he stopped having any thoughts whatsoever, about Tanya or anyone.

Some days, though, it was as if a ray of light broke through to the inside. It would happen in the mornings. Images would appear in his head. A man in a coat drawing a car in the snow with a stick. Papa? A woman lying on the sofa, snuggled up under a blanket. Mama? Her features were hidden by her hair falling over her face. A little girl feeding the birds, pouring crumbs into a bird feeder on the windowsill outside. Who was that? And a little boy in woollen tights? Shura felt anxious, sensing that he ought to know who these people were, but couldn't remember.

But then they were taken to breakfast. And after the grey porridge and the grey bread, that anxiety disappeared – like a niggling splinter being pulled out – and so too did the memories.

The days and nights ticked by at an even pace, like the minute hand of the clock.

Until one day something happened . . .

It was supper-time. The banner on the wall proclaimed its stern reminder: WHEN I EAT, I AM DEAF AND MUTE. The cooks scurried about with their pots between the rows of tables. Spoons clattered away. Shura lowered his into the grey porridge.

Somewhere in the corridor a scream rang out like a shot. The clatter of spoons stopped. The children's heads all rose as one. Even the cooks stopped in their tracks.

'She bit me, the wretch!' yelped Big Nose.

'Everyone stay in your seats!' ordered Bollard. With her ruler in her hand, she rushed into the corridor to help, leaving the door wide open in her hurry.

The kerfuffle could be heard from where Shura sat: the noise of stomping, of puffing and panting. Shura saw Bollard and Big Nose dragging the girl past the doorway, as she dug her heels in, trying to resist.

Shura's heart skipped a beat: *Tanya!* And then the thumping started again: no, it wasn't Tanya.

The girl's hair was half chopped off. Tufts stuck out here and there.

'It's a mistake!' cried the girl, trying to wriggle free. 'I'm not an enemy! I'm a Pioneer! My papa hasn't done anything! None of us have! I'll write to Comrade Stalin! It's a mistake! Let me go!'

Bollard and Big Nose struggled to restrain her, grabbing at her arm, then her leg. From the side it looked like the three of them were performing some kind of strange dance. The screams gradually died down, until one final echo rang through the corridor. Then everything was silent.

Once again, the room was filled with cooks holding pans with tea towels wrapped round the handles, their hats seeming to float through the steam. Spoons began to clatter.

'Did you hear that?' exclaimed Shura, his voice raised above the normal whisper. 'Zoya? Mitya? Anya? Did you hear that?'

Suddenly he stared at the table; a piece of bread had disappeared from his plate. *How can that be?* Shura turned his head.

'That was you!' he gasped.

Next to him, Zoya-Ninel's jaws were hard at work, her cheeks quivering as she chewed as fast as she could. The guilty, frightened look on her face said it all. Shura was stunned. The girl gulped down the stolen bread. Shura stared at his glass of murky tea.

'Give him another piece,' one cook shouted to another.

'Another piece?' the second cook yelled. 'The state squanders enough on these enemies. Sitting around getting fat at the state's expense! He'll make do without!'

Everyone looked down at their plates, focusing on the

movement of their spoons. The banner on the wall caught Shura's eye: WHEN I EAT, I AM DEAF AND MUTE.

Bollard burst in noisily through the door. She was pressing a grey piece of cloth against her hand.

'Still eating, you savages? Well, eat, then, since the state is so generous as to feed you,' she growled as she unwound the cloth; the girl had bitten her, too. 'You don't deserve to be fed, and yet . . .'

Seeing that girl struggling suddenly unleashed Shura's thoughts. *A mistake.* That's what he'd heard her shout. *Mistake? Is it possible? Well, then, I'm here by mistake as well! I'm not an enemy of the state. And neither are Mama, Papa and Bobka . . . They're not enemies . . . Papa! Mama! Tanya! . . . I have to find them.*

He was so distracted by this flood of thoughts that he completely forgot to be annoyed about the bread.

'Zoya,' he said softly.

A quick glance, her eyes like two mice darting back and forth.

'It wasn't me!' she lied, as she quickly gulped down her mouthful. 'I didn't take it!'

'Oh no – I don't care about that.'

Zoya rushed to finish her portion. Her eyes were drawn to Shura's plate. 'Can I eat yours, then? If you don't want it?'

'Why are you here?' asked Shura.

'I don't know. I suppose I have to be here.'

'Your mama and papa aren't enemies.'

'If I'm here, that means they're enemies,' Zoya-Ninel answered without emotion. 'They don't punish innocent people.'

'It's not like you think,' whispered Shura.

'I'm hu-u-ungry,' she whimpered.

'Silence!' Bollard pounced on them, bellowing in Shura's ear, *When I eat, I am deaf and mute!*

Zoya quickly swapped his full plate for her empty one and set to work with her spoon, greedily shovelling the gruel into her mouth.

All the others pointedly turned away.

Shura obediently drank up his tea, which had gone cold, and then got up with everyone else and marched off to bed.

The next morning they were taken back to the dining room as usual. Shura was hungry, after missing his dinner the night before, and struggled to keep up, his huge boots constantly slipping off his feet. Falling out of the line, he suddenly saw the column of children from the side: all dressed in identical grey pyjamas, all with shaved heads, which made their ears and eyes especially prominent. Shura couldn't distinguish Anya, Zoya or Mitya.

And me? What about me? he thought. *I'm the same. Tanya will never recognize me!*

At the table, as he scraped the bowl with his spoon, for a moment he glimpsed Tanya's face at the bottom – he was sure of it! But then the grey, slimy gruel slithered back and it was gone.

Suddenly someone pinched him painfully in the back. Shura turned to the right, to the left, but no – they were all chewing, staring ahead with eyes glazed over. And when he turned back to his plate, his bread was gone.

Shura did everything he could to distract himself from thinking about food. But hunger dug its claws into his stomach.

In the sewing room, the machines rattled away. Shura turned the handle of his machine. His stomach ached with hunger. The dusty smell of the sackcloth wafted into his nostrils. The light glistened dimly on the rows of shaved heads bent over their work.

'Zoya,' whispered Shura but loudly enough for her to hear him.

All of a sudden, two eyes opened in the wall. They stared straight at Shura. The look was piercing and lifeless at the same time.

Shura flinched and quickly looked down at the sackcloth creeping along under his needle.

But when he – cautiously – looked up again, the eyes were gone. The wall was an ordinary wall. Greyish-green on the bottom half, greyish-yellow on the top half.

Shura suddenly remembered hearing about how Arctic explorers would see visions when they were starving. *Hallucinations! That's what they were called.* Shura realized that this was the same. The explorers had needed to summon all their willpower to get through the hunger. *They managed, and so will I*, Shura told himself. *And maybe I'll even get out of here.*

'Zoya,' Shura whispered again, under the cover of the background hum, facing her skinny, hunched-over back. 'I'm not cross about the bread. Honest – Soviet promise!'

Her back straightened slightly. She was listening.

'Zoya.' Shura took a breath and then whispered something, an idea that was forming in his head just as he was about to say it. He lowered his voice even more quietly this time: 'Zoya, let's escape.'

'Why?' she asked, indifferently. Her back hunched over her sewing again.

Shura thought he saw eyes staring at him from the wall again, but in another spot this time. He squeezed his eyes shut. *Ugh! Creepy!* He took a deep breath and reminded himself it was just a hallucination. He opened his eyes again. Of course, there was nothing on the wall.

'Zoya . . .'

A pause.

'How?'

'I've got a plan.'

She listened.

'The main thing is we do it together. One of us pushes the other up first. Then that person pulls the second one up. Through the window.'

'And then what?' Zoya whispered.

'STALCHIL!' Bollard appeared out of nowhere. 'Get up!'

Shura jumped off his chair, stood to attention and stared straight ahead.

'Who were you talking to?'

'No one.'

'Answer me!'

'I wasn't talking to anyone.'

'In that case . . .' Bollard lightly tapped the ruler against the palm of her hand.

'I was talking to myself,' Shura insisted.

'Ninel!' Bollard barked in a terrifying voice that made everyone look up. The rattling of the sewing machines ceased.

Zoya slowly stood up. Her skinny neck protruded pitifully from her gaping collar. Her ears were ablaze on her shaved head.

'Hands out,' Bollard ordered.

'I was talking to myself!' shouted Shura.

'Hands out! Straight ahead.'

Shura and Zoya-Ninel stretched their hands forward, their outspread fingers trembling. The ruler rose up in the air. It slammed down flat on Zoya's hands – again and again. Tears streamed slowly and silently down Zoya's cheeks. They also punished you if you screamed.

Bollard took a few steps back. She took a bigger swing this time. The ruler whistled through the air. Shura squeezed his eyes shut, knowing it was his turn next. He clenched his teeth.

Smack!

Zoya screamed. Shura didn't feel the blow, and opened his eyes in surprise. A broad stripe had appeared on Zoya's neck, scarlet and swollen, where the ruler had lashed her.

'Now is everything clear?' Bollard gave the ashen-faced children a leaden stare, like a boa constrictor to a mouse. She didn't lay a finger on Shura.

The bell rang. Everyone got up. They placed the covers over the sewing machines and started to form a queue.

'Zoya!' Shura squeezed in behind her.

She didn't answer.

'I'm sorry. Does it hurt?'

Silence.

'Ninel,' Shura tried.

Anya-Octobrina silently shoved him with her shoulder, pushing him out of the queue.

'But, I . . . Anya!'

Mitya-Vors turned his back on Shura without a word. One by one, they all turned their backs on him.

'I didn't do it on purpose. Honestly!'

Shura was pushed back to the end of the line.

'Guys!'

But the only answer he got was grey backs turned towards him. No one would speak to Shura. No one wanted to stand beside him.

'March!' ordered Bollard.

Boots shuffling, the column inched along the corridor to the dining room. In the dining room, everyone tried to keep a distance from Shura. They weren't allowed to swap seats, but Zoya, Mitya and Anya all turned to face away, as if recoiling from him. They looked down at their porridge.

'Zoya . . . Anya . . . Guys . . .' Shura was so wounded he could barely eat. There was a lump in his throat, and tears welled up in his eyes.

I wonder if I'll be able to sleep, Shura thought, pulling the grey blanket around himself.

'Oh!' He opened his eyes with a start. The dorm was dark. Suddenly his mind was flooded with brightly coloured images. Mama in a green silk dress. Papa doing his exercises. Tanya reading, nibbling a cracker. His bed. A reed screen. Bobka sitting on the potty. Tanya's violin. A door. The street. A door. Mama. Papa. Bobka. Tanya. Bobka. Papa. Tanya. Mama.

Shura jolted upright. Sleep hovered over the rows of grey beds. He was suddenly aware of the sound of the children's breathing: they all inhaled and exhaled together, as if on command.

He lay down again. Carefully, as if pressing a fresh flower to his chest. He started to recall the colourful images.

A moonbeam slid through the window. Identical beds in a row. Identical grey mounds. Shura felt uneasy for a moment; he imagined this was a cemetery. Even the headboards of the beds were like gravestones.

Shura sat up again, breathing heavily. A drop of sweat slid down his back. Now he could make out the identically shaved heads in the darkness. He heard people breathing and snoring. But he was no longer calm, his heart was turning somersaults in his chest.

He threw back the blanket, got up and walked silently across the bedroom. He didn't know what he was doing, but lying there in the dark was unbearable.

He carefully opened the door. The corridor stretched in both directions like long empty sleeves. It was dark and quiet. Grey squares of moonlight fell on the floor from the unpainted halves of the windows. Shura carefully avoided stepping on them, just in case.

From a distance came a bumping sound, like someone

rolling a potato on the roof. He waited until it stopped. Then there was another. And another. The noise was getting closer and closer. It became deafening. It didn't sound like a rolling potato any more. It was more like an aeroplane trying to start up.

Shura froze. He reached a turn in the corridor. Shura pressed himself against the wall, then crouched down quietly, on all fours, and peered cautiously round the corner.

There was Bollard, asleep on a chair, her head thrown back and her bollard-legs outstretched. Her mouth was open, and her noxious breath emerged in bursts between every snore. A table lamp with a green shade cast an unnecessary circle of light. A key lay in the spotlight. Bollard's huge hands pressed a book to her stomach.

Then there was a shudder as the warden woke up with a snort and a jerk of her legs. The book fluttered in her hands. Something rectangular slid out from among the pages. Shura darted back round the corner and watched as the object gently wafted to the floor.

It landed face up and Shura saw that it was a photograph. A young lady in a huge hat, as big as a wheel, with white roses. The photograph must have been old: the image had yellowed a little with age, and nobody wore hats like that any more, probably not since tsarist times.

Shura pressed himself against the wall. The picture had landed in a pale circle of light. Shura was in the dark. His heart was pounding, drowning out the warden's heavy footsteps.

Bollard reached down to pick up the photograph. Shura

looked at the hand, which looked so strange, with chubby fingers like the tentacles of a cuttlefish. The photograph and this podgy hand belonged to two different worlds.

Two staring eyes suddenly appeared on the wall above the photograph. Shura held his breath. His drowsy eyes were wandering helplessly and squinting to try to focus. His knees felt weak, his back was soaked with sweat. Silently he prayed that they wouldn't see him.

. . .

'Tanya, you don't believe me, do you?'

'I do believe you. Of course I believe you. It's just . . .'

'They were absolutely human eyes!'

'It's just that sometimes people invent things.'

'They lie?'

Tanya shook her head. 'Not necessarily. Or rather, yes, but not intentionally to fool everyone. Or to make people listen. Sometimes people just don't understand what's going on, so they explain things as best they can, and then they believe their own explanation. Like we believed that the birds could talk to us.'

'But they did talk to us!'

Tanya was silent. 'Now I'm not so sure.'

'Why would I lie?' asked Shura, offended.

'I'm not saying that you're lying! But . . . sometimes it helps to think something up and play along, in order to hide from what is really the case.'

'But I did see them!'

. . .

He really did see them, those eyes.

Bollard's hand quickly snatched the photograph. The eyes burst wide open, a split second too late. The eyes looked up, apparently staring in Bollard's direction. They were wide awake by now. Cold, alert, piercing.

Shura heard Bollard singing quietly.

The sound couldn't be more different from her usual rhinoceros roar! She was singing a lullaby. 'Ah-ah, ah-ah . . .' she warbled.

Her voice was creepy, as if Bollard were rocking a venomous snake off to sleep.

The eyes on the wall twitched, then glazed over again sleepily. For a few seconds Shura saw them struggle: an angry, merciless glare came to the surface, then they twitched again before succumbing to the veil of sleep. Finally, the eyes dozed off, and disappeared.

Bollard stood a little longer, softly singing. She paused, then tiptoed away and returned to her seat. The chair creaked under her mighty body. The book slammed shut, swallowing up the mysterious photograph.

The silence seemed endless. But then, eventually, the snoring sounded like an aeroplane engine struggling to restart: '*grrrrrrrr*', pause, '*grrrrrrrr*', pause, '*grrrrrrrr*'.

Shura slipped noiselessly round the corner. He crept past the sleeping warden. He quietly took the key and lowered it into his pocket.

He couldn't help himself, and silently opened the book. There she was: the girl in the hat. He tucked the photograph into the top of his pyjamas. The warden grunted.

Shura quickly stepped out of the spotlit circle into the

darkness, where he froze. Everything was quiet. Squeezing up against the wall, he crept down the corridor.

What am I doing? thought Shura, shocked at himself. *Get back to the bedroom before it's too late!* But he knew: it was already too late.

In a square of grey moonlight, he noticed a shadow. A rat. She also noticed him. She stood on her hind legs and sniffed. The moonlight turned her whiskers into a silver halo.

Politeness works wonders, Shura remembered Tanya saying. If birds could talk, then perhaps . . .

'Esteemed rat, would you please spare me a little of your precious time?'

The rat snorted and swayed from side to side. She was giggling.

'Precious time? Esteemed rat? Hee hee. Very cute.' She licked her paw and patted her whiskers. 'But compliments don't fill you up when you're hungry.'

'I have nothing else to offer you,' answered Shura honestly.

'I know,' said the rat. 'I know everything here. I know even more than they do. Shhh . . . They're everywhere.'

'Dearest rat,' he whispered softly. 'All I have is this key.' Shura raised it to show her. 'Perhaps it's for the pantry? It'll be full of grain and butter, and lots of other things.'

'And why would you be interested in helping me find food?'

'Please help me get out of here.'

'Where to?' The rat was genuinely amazed.

'Just out of here.' Shura waved his hand.

'Why?' The rat flinched, and her whiskers fluttered. She

stared at him, puzzled. 'What's wrong with it here? They feed you, they dress you.'

Shura said nothing. It would be impolite to say the truth: the rat lived here, too, after all.

The rat continued animatedly, 'There's a roof over your head. They teach you how to use the sewing machines. You should be grateful. They take care of you. You don't need to worry about a thing.'

'Take care of us?' exclaimed Shura. 'Take care?'

'Shhh,' hissed the rat, looking up suddenly. She froze, only her ears and whiskers twitching. But the wall was deaf and blind.

'No one gives me bread on a plate,' said the rat with feeling.

'Help me, please,' Shura repeated.

'You're a fool. Running away from happiness.' She sighed. But her eyes were ablaze, twinkling with greedy thoughts of food. 'OK, give me the key.'

The rat tested the key with a little nibble. 'Mmm, yes it might be for the pantry. And if not . . . well, it doesn't matter – we rats can always scavenge a little something. We don't turn anything down! Come on, then!' And she dashed off into the darkness, her body undulating as she ran. Shura could barely keep up.

They scarpered past the clothes store. Rows of identical clothes hung on identical hangers. Shura yanked a coat off a hanger and grabbed a hat. His other hand deftly snatched a pair of boots. And he thrust a pair of mittens into his pocket.

The corridor stretched before them like a black tunnel. At

the next corner, the rat suddenly stopped. Shura almost trod on her tail.

The rat pointed with her paw at the wall. In the grey moonlight, Shura saw something emerging from the wall, two oval shapes, unfurling like the leaves of a ficus tree. Ears.

Shura gulped.

The rat gestured with her paw across her throat, then crossed her paws in front of her nose, as if to say, *That's it, I'm done.*

Shura, holding his breath, pulled a mitten out of his pocket. He tiptoed past the rat. Slowly, as though moving through water, he swung the mitt and flung it down the corridor. It slid along the floor, rustling as it went. The ears twisted around towards the noise. And Shura and the rat tiptoed away in the opposite direction.

'Phew, that was lucky,' whispered the rat once they had reached a safe distance.

Finally, the rat stopped next to a door. Shura took the opportunity to catch his breath. He started to pull on the boots.

'Hey, fool!' said the rat impatiently. 'Who's going to unlock it?'

'You've got the key.'

'Fool! I can't reach.'

Shura took the key from the rat. He turned it in the keyhole. The door flew open.

Shura stared in amazement, his hands dropping to his sides. Before his eyes appeared a dense, whitish-grey mist. It seemed to flow, swirling like milk poured into hot tea.

The rat finally managed to jump high enough to grasp the

key, pulling it out of the lock, and they fell to the floor together; the key rattled, the rat landed with a thud.

Fog was not an uncommon sight in Leningrad, but Shura had never seen anything like this before. He felt uneasy.

'I can take you back to your dorm if you've changed your mind,' suggested the rat.

Shura shook his head.

The rat pawed the the key. 'Well, fine. If someone's a fool, there's nothing I can do about it.'

'And where will I find the Raven?'

'Oh, you really are a fool!'

'Yes, you've said that!' Shura was indignant. 'Would you please just tell me which way to go!'

'They'll find you.'

The fog ahead seemed as dense as a soufflé, as though you had to scoop your way through it with a spoon.

'Keep going straight ahead. And don't be afraid,' said the rat.

'What is there to be afraid of?' Shura peered into the fog, but, try as he might, he couldn't see anything or anyone.

The door banged softly behind him.

Shura turned round. But the door was already obscured by the fog.

He stood still for a moment. Then he stretched out his hands in front of him, to avoid bumping into anything unexpected. And carefully he walked forward. Slowly at first, then gradually faster.

Then he ran.

Straight ahead.

CHAPTER EIGHT

There was no end to the fog. It seemed to go on forever. Shura quickly lost sense of time. He had no idea how long he had spent walking, his arms stretched forward, staring helplessly into the whitish misty air. His feet pounded hard on the tarmac.

Gradually Shura started to see pale-blue patches of light overhead, fuzzy through the fog. After a while he could see dim lights far ahead, as the fog started to thin. Houses began to tower above him, to his left and right: dark, looming silhouettes. Somewhere in the distance he heard a gentle splashing sound – the river? Every now and then he saw a lonely window lit up in one of the houses, and, without knowing why, Shura crouched down and crept along against the wall.

No one was following him.

Shura realized that he was walking along the embankment. Only he didn't recognize it to begin with. The houses seemed to shiver in the chilly dawn half-light. Shura noticed only a few wrinkled, brown leaves on the trees.

'It's autumn!' He was amazed. 'How long was I there, at the Grey House?'

The last time he'd seen the trees, they were trembling in the March breeze. Since then, the trees had blossomed, grown leaves, enjoyed the summer and then lost their leaves in the autumn winds. It seemed like barely a week had passed, perhaps a couple. What if it had actually been more than a year? Two? Three?

'What if I'm already ten?'

Shura closed his eyes in horror.

By now the fog clung only in dips and hollows. A large harvest moon gazed down from the sky. Beyond the river's granite wall loomed a bulky shape, flickering with glints of light. In the distance, beyond the heavy splash of water, Shura could just make out a tarnished golden spire, faintly reflecting a glimmer of moonlight.

It was the Peter and Paul Fortress! Shura rejoiced as though it were an old friend. From there it was just a stone's throw to his aunt's. And then they would all sit down together and figure out what to do next. Shura had a spring in his step now, eagerly looking in the distance for the bridge to the other side to emerge from the fog.

But the strange thing was that the spire didn't get any closer; if anything it seemed to be getting further away. Shura quickened his pace. The spire got smaller and smaller, until it was minuscule. It was like looking through the wrong end of the binoculars. Yet the embankment still looked the same.

What's going on? The faster I walk, the further it is to go.

Ahead he spotted a hunched figure in a coat and mittens. And further on, another and another.

'Hi!' shouted Shura.

One woman turned round. 'Hush,' she whispered in fright. 'What are you doing, boy?'

'I'm looking for . . .' Shura began.

'Shhh!' she exclaimed in a whisper. 'I know. I know what you're looking for. Just don't shout. The woman you need's over there, see? With the briefcase. There . . .' She waved her hand towards the river.

Shura had no idea what she meant. But he went up to the woman with the briefcase. She stood leaning her back against the wall.

'Sorry to disturb you,' Shura began.

The woman turned slowly to face him. She gave him a weary look then shook her head. Taking off her mitten (Shura was surprised to see so many people in mittens) and blowing on her fingers, she pulled out of her briefcase a battered notebook with a pen tucked inside. She opened it and noted something down.

'You're number five hundred and eighteen.' Her voice seemed frozen, lifeless.

Shura wanted to yell, 'What for? What number?' But, before he could speak, the woman grasped his hand and, pressing her pen into his palm so hard it hurt, she wrote three large digits in purple ink: 518.

'Who are you?' Shura shouted. He was angry, but his voice came out sounding thin and pathetic.

'Go, go,' the woman with the briefcase waved at him. 'Don't just stand there.'

Another woman came up to him from behind. 'Come here, boy. You're behind me.'

Shura joined her. They walked away from the water's edge. The woman headed slowly towards the big buildings that emerged from the fog, standing identically straight and tall.

Why are they all wearing mittens in autumn? He longed to ask someone.

Everybody must be asleep – there were no lights on anywhere. Except for one building where all the windows were lit. The building was huge, tall, black, awkward.

'My son's been arrested. I've come to ask about him . . . And bring him something to eat,' the woman explained, raising her basket slightly to show him. 'They said he's a spy. But he doesn't even know any foreign languages.'

In the Grey House they told us our parents were spies! thought Shura, alarmed when he made the connection. Was this where the Raven was keeping his prisoners, then? Perhaps he was on the right track to finding Mama and Papa!

'My parents were taken away,' Shura told the lady, 'but *my* mama and papa didn't do anything wrong.' He placed extra stress on the word 'my'.

'If they're not guilty, they'll look into it,' she reassured him wearily, looking up at the glowing windows, blurred in the fog. 'This is the headquarters.'

Did that mean this great black building was the Raven's nest? All this time he was looking for the Raven to ask for his mama and papa back, and this was where he needed to be all along?

They stood and looked at the windows. Occasionally a shadow flitted by in one window or another.

'We can't go any closer,' said the woman. 'They don't like it when people come at night.'

'Who are *they*? Is there more than one Raven?'

'Shhh. Let's carry on and pretend that we're just out walking.'

She picked up the basket with a sigh. Shura would have offered to help. But maybe her son was a spy. Hard to believe, but still . . .

The woman walked slowly along the pavement. Shura unbuttoned his coat but didn't follow her. All around them, shadowy shapes swayed in the dark. Gradually these shapes became more solid and it became clear that they were people in coats, thick scarves and hats.

All he heard was people asking, 'What's your number?'

'And you?'

'Is there anyone over fifty?'

'Over three hundred?'

'Where are the one hundreds?'

'Anyone here in the two hundreds?'

Hushed whispers rustled on all sides. Grey figures emerged from the darkness . . . women, children . . . wrapped up tight in warm winter clothes. So many of them! Shura felt scared when he realized he was surrounded by so many people.

They gradually took their places in the queue, one after another. *So, are all these women waiting to see the Raven?* As he looked around him, it started to dawn on Shura that they must be the mothers of spies, the relatives of people who had been arrested like his mama and papa. So, did that mean that these girls were the sisters of spies? Of enemies of the state?

That these women who were standing here in their hundreds were the wives and mothers of saboteurs and infiltrators, people who had been plotting to harm our country and our citizens? Did all these women wake up one day and find that their loved ones had been keeping secrets from them? Living a lie and plotting sabotage . . . until the day they were arrested and their relatives learnt the truth?

Shura couldn't see any malice on the women's faces, only exhaustion and sadness. Their loved ones must have been cruel to cause them all this trouble.

And suddenly he thought, what about his mama and papa? What if they hadn't told him everything? What if he didn't know everything about them?

Shura felt like ice was spreading through his insides as he struggled with this thought. It became difficult to breathe. And women kept coming and taking their places, one behind the other in the line.

'What's your number?'

'And you?'

. . . *Could what they said in the Grey House be true? Could it?* Like all parents, Shura's sometimes went out in the evenings. Where did they go? Did children really ever know anything about their mama and papa?

'And you, boy? What's your number?' An old woman in a thick grey coat approached Shura. She pulled off her glove with her teeth and stretched out her bony hand. A three-digit number was written on her palm.

A short distance away he saw a little boy hugging his mother's leg, wrapped up like a small bundle with a warm shawl tied diagonally across his chest. He stared blankly at Shura.

'What's your number? Don't you know your number?' the old woman kept asking.

'Boy, show your number,' others from the queue began to ask.

Shura couldn't utter a word. His head was spinning.

The little boy stared at him with big round eyes.

But what about Bobka . . . ? Did that mean Bobka was a spy, too? That's madness! How could he be? He's a toddler who can't even talk! And yet he also disappeared . . .

Shura's thoughts galloped and collided. He staggered and swayed, but the people steadied him. After looking at his palm, they showed him his place in the queue: behind a lady in a checked coat and in front of an old woman with a wart on her long nose. Ahead were just backs, backs, backs . . .

Shura quickly grew tired of standing and waiting. He was numb through and through from the cold and from standing still. *So that's why they're all wearing winter mittens in autumn!* he guessed. *They must stand here waiting for hours on end.*

People shifted their weight from foot to foot, trying to convince themselves that the queue was moving. But if they shuffled forward too much, they only got bunched up and the ones in front snapped at them angrily.

'Don't push!'

'Careful!'

Time ticked by slowly and they still hadn't opened up the Black Raven's lair. *The Raven's nest? It's a building, so I guess it's the Raven's House.*

More time went by, and still there was no movement. Shura had run out of thoughts and was fed up of standing there waiting.

Up in front, there was a kink in the queue. The adults were craning their necks to see the house.

Ahead of him in the queue, Shura saw a little girl in a knitted hat. She was about the same height as him. Unlike other boys, Shura didn't hate girls and he wasn't scared of them. He had a sister, after all. He knew how to be friends with girls. But he didn't have anything to start a conversation about. No marbles, no ball, no bicycle. Well, almost nothing! He remembered Bollard's photograph. Little girls loved princesses. The lady in the hat was like something out of a fairy tale: you'd never see anyone like her on the street. Shura raised his arm and stuck his hand inside the top of his coat. He shivered as the cold slipped in. He fumbled around and found the photograph's hard edge. He put the picture in his outside pocket. It felt warm from the warmth of his body.

'Hello. Do you want to play?' Shura asked the little girl politely.

She looked at him, but said nothing. Perhaps she didn't have a brother, and she was afraid of the boys in her yard. Shura wasn't offended. After all, she didn't know that he was just trying to be friendly.

'I have a photograph. Do you want to see it?'

The girl took a few steps towards him. Shura held out the photograph to show her. She stretched her neck and squinted, staring at the strange hat.

Suddenly a skinny woman in a scarf jerked her hand and

pulled the girl away from Shura. The woman's face twisted into a scowl. She looked at Shura with disgust and malice, as though he were a loathsome cockroach.

'What are you doing?' the skinny woman screamed at her daughter. 'Have you gone mad?' Her voice fell to a whisper, a barely audible hiss. 'We're surrounded by spies here. Do you understand? Enemies of the people. Do you understand?' Every time she said 'understand' she shook her daughter by the hand. 'Do you want people to think you're one, too?'

'And you,' muttered Shura.

'What did you say?' the woman snarled. But she didn't raise her voice.

The girl looked at Shura with fright. Her fear hurt Shura more than if she'd said something nasty. He tucked the photograph inside his cap, in the front. He squeezed back in the queue between the checked-coat lady and the old woman with the wart. He felt sick inside. The criss-cross pattern of the checked fabric reminded him of prison bars.

How could I be a spy? thought Shura. *I'm not a spy.* His thoughts rushed about again, clattering into one another. Shura tried desperately to make sense of it all. He felt that he was on the verge of making some important connection, but he couldn't quite keep up with his own thoughts.

She thinks I'm a spy. I think she's a spy. And we all think that about each other.

Suddenly he felt a jolt from behind. The crowd was pushing forward. An impatient wave ran through the queue. Everybody craned their necks to see what was happening.

There, up ahead, a little hatch had opened in the wall. A small semicircular window, like a little mouth. It was quite low down so the grown-up at the front was having to bend down to speak into it. *It must be intended for children*, Shura thought; it looked like it would be at his eye level. *Strange . . .*

But he didn't have time to finish his thought.

'Spy!' a woman cried. 'She's pushing in!'

Pushing and shoving, huffing and puffing. It looked like punches were being thrown.

'I just need to find out about my husband!'

'Vermin!'

'Wait in turn like everyone else!'

'I don't need to stand in line! My husband isn't a spy! He isn't guilty! He hasn't done anything!'

'Don't you dare push in!'

Shura heard the sound of fabric ripping and women shouting. The grown-ups in the queue all craned their necks inquisitively. But the women were quickly separated.

The woman who had tried to push in dragged herself despondently back down the line. She was carrying a basket. Her hat was skew-whiff and the collar of her coat was half torn-off. She was crying. People turned away.

'I won't have it!' cried the wretched-looking woman with the basket. Her ripped collar made her look scruffy and down-trodden. 'My husband is not a spy. He was taken by mistake.'

Shura jumped when he heard that. *What? By mistake? So, mistakes do happen, then?*

'I've written a letter! To Comrade Raven personally! Dear citizens, please let me into the queue,' the woman begged.

Shura's hands started to sweat. A letter? A letter to the Raven! That's what he needed to do! Of course! After all, his mama and papa hadn't done anything either.

Suddenly it all seemed so simple. It was a mistake! Of course!

'Go ahead, write your letters,' a woman towards the front hissed back at her. 'At the end of the queue!' She muttered, 'Honestly, who does she think she is?'

Shura trembled. He decided to run and catch up with the woman with the basket. But when he tried to move he was squeezed forward. Then he was squeezed backwards again. Shura took a deep breath and then, arms outstretched, launched himself at the huge, scratchy coat in front. The coat stood firm as a wall.

The woman with the torn-off collar was getting further and further away. Shura pushed the coat in front of him and the one behind him, and wrenched himself out of the line.

'Where are you going? You'll lose your place!' several people shouted after him.

He ran towards the woman. He kept running. She was pressing a crumpled handkerchief against her nose. It was spotted with red. She had clearly been injured in the fight.

'So, you can send a letter?' he asked breathlessly as he caught up with her.

She sniffed. 'What do you want?' she snapped, in a nasal voice.

'My mama and papa and baby brother were also taken . . . by mistake.'

The woman looked at him with a morose expression.

'Honestly! They're not spies! It's a mistake!'

She carried on walking, looking down at the ground.

Shura followed, keeping up at her side. 'Please!'

The woman stopped abruptly.

'Auntie, how do I send a letter?'

The woman wiped her eyes. She patted her nose again, then slipped the handkerchief into her pocket. She took a deep breath.

'Auntie, please help me!'

She rummaged in her handbag and fished out first a sheet of paper, then an envelope, then a pen. She clicked the clasp shut, then offered Shura the paper and pen. He hesitated.

'Umm, my handwriting isn't very good. What if I smudge the ink? It's a serious matter!' he began to explain, feeling himself blush. He imagined her stepping away and yelling, '*He can't even write, so he crawls to me for help!*'

But the woman only sighed. 'Tell me what to write.' She pressed the paper against her hard handbag and held the pen ready.

What a kind lady, thought Shura, relieved. *Wonderful. Soon everything will be sorted out.*

'Your husband will be home soon, too!' he promised confidently. 'He's not guilty of anything, and they don't put innocent people in jail. Please write: "Comrade Raven!"'

Then Shura looked at the sheet and grabbed the woman's hand.

'What?'

'Wait.' Perhaps the Raven didn't like being addressed as 'Raven'. Otherwise, why did people always talk about him only in a whisper, always looking over their shoulders like that? 'Just write "Comrade".'

The woman nodded.

The tone needed to be functional and firm. Shura frowned as he dictated: ' "I need my mama and papa to come home. They were taken by mistake. And where's Bobka?" ' He explained to the woman: 'That's my brother. But don't write that. Carry on: "Please make the necessary arrangements as soon as possible. It's time for us to go home." '

The pen scratched softly against the paper. Shura thought about what to add. He remembered Auntie Rita. ' "And give us our rooms back!" '

'Is that it?' asked the woman.

'Er . . . yes.'

'You need to sign it.' She held out the pen.

With an important expression on his face, Shura scribbled his name at the bottom. Grown-ups' signatures were always completely illegible, after all. He folded the letter in half. The woman stood right by him, her whole body stooping forward, like an old horse.

'Done!' Shura exclaimed.

She looked at him with her puffy red eyes.

'Write on the envelope: "Into his hands personally." No, actually: "Into his beak." No, wait,' Shura hastily interrupted himself. He thought for a moment. The Raven would probably prefer to be addressed like a person, Shura realized. He felt sure of it. 'Just write: "Into his hands personally." '

The woman addressed the envelope and handed it to Shura. He quickly licked the gum and pressed it tightly to seal it.

'Have you sent yours yet?'

She shook her head. She blew her nose. She shrugged her shoulders.

'Give it to me – I'll take both!'

She paused for a moment, then undid the clasp on her bag to take it out.

'I'll be right back.' Shura snatched the thin, oblong envelope from her hand. He tucked the letters into the top of his coat.

'Don't worry. Into his hands personally!' He took off his cap. 'Hold it please. To be on the safe side.'

Confused, the woman pressed his cap to her stomach.

'In case I get into a fight,' Shura explained, unwrapping his scarf to hand to her. He undid the buttons on his collar and unfastened it. 'So it doesn't get torn off.'

The woman nodded. Her long face and brown eyes also made her look like a gentle, weary horse.

Do horses cry? Shura suddenly wondered. He chased the thought away and laughed. Why should he be afraid? Why should he run away from everyone? After all, he wasn't guilty of anything! Shura straightened his shoulders. The woman couldn't help but smile.

Shura set off running towards the Raven's House, to the front of the queue.

The sky was now light, but it still looked like a pane of thick, cloudy glass.

The lights were still on in the Raven's windows, but they seemed dimmer. The queue still didn't seem to be moving. Shura trotted along beside it. *Hmm, what can I do so they'll let me in at the front of the line?*

'Mama,' he whimpered every now and then for sympathy, turning his head to look around. 'Have you seen my mama?'

It worked! No one answered him, but they didn't stop him either.

As he approached the little hatch in the wall, the queue was so dense that it was more like a crowd. Shura pressed his elbows against his body and crouched down to plunge through the forest of legs. Someone gasped as he bumped into them, another person yelped, someone stepped on his hand. Shura crawled forward, twisting this way and that, scurrying along on his hands and feet.

The screams and grumbles were always behind him; they swore at him but they couldn't stop him just by shouting. The people were standing so closely together that they couldn't bend down and catch him by the collar.

A warm, dusty breeze blew from somewhere. Shura dodged a briefcase, which nearly bashed him in the temple. He found himself face-to-face with some brand-new, knee-high boots with chrome trim. All the other shoes, boots and galoshes were standing with toes pointing towards the Black Raven's lair. But these ones were pointing in the opposite direction. They were very shiny.

Shura's instinct was to make a run for it. But he didn't have time.

He was grabbed from the ground, picked up by the scruff of his neck.

The queue gasped. The woman bent over at the hatch froze.

'What do you think you're playing at? Get back in line! If

you make him angry, he'll shut the hatch!' Shura heard people shouting from along the queue.

Shura's feet felt the tarmac. The hand released Shura's collar and brushed down his knees. As the man straightened up, his hand flew up to his cap with a blue band in salute.

'Shhh,' the tall, kind-looking soldier said loudly. 'The child was nearly crushed.'

The people in the queue turned away or looked down at their feet.

'Boy, who do you belong to?' The soldier looked over Shura's head into the crowd. 'Citizens, who has lost this child?'

Shura stretched out his legs, and threw up his palm to salute the soldier.

'I'm not lost. I'm on my own.'

Tanya and I ran away, so everyone presumed we were to blame. No need to run away if you've got nothing to hide. And people won't chase after you, he thought to himself.

And in fact the soldier in the cap didn't shout at him or blow his whistle, but squatted down to listen to him.

'Oh?' he said.

'Comrade, I have a serious matter to attend to.'

'What's that, then?' said the soldier.

Shura pulled out the two letters from inside his coat.

'For Comrade Raven, personally.'

The queue gasped in horror. Shura felt a sudden icy draught against his back as he sensed their fear.

Shura jutted out his chin defiantly. *Are they afraid? Fine! Let them be afraid. They're all spies, saboteurs, enemies of the state.*

Well, they *might be – but I'm not, and neither are my brother, my papa or my mama.*

Shura looked the soldier straight in the eye. The soldier stood up without a word. He took both letters.

But, despite his outward confidence, inside Shura couldn't help but panic. *This is crazy. He's going to rip the letters to shreds!* After all, how could the soldier know that Shura was an honest Soviet citizen? When everywhere around them were the relatives of criminals, and for all he knew they might all be as bad as their loved ones who had been arrested.

But it seemed the soldier could tell Shura was a good person.

'Of course,' answered the soldier. His voice was not in the slightest bit angry.

Shura breathed a sigh of relief. The soldier opened the door behind him a crack – Shura again smelt the warm, dusty aroma of the room – and pulled out a plump grey sack. Shura had an unpleasant, prickly feeling for a moment when he recognized the bag: it was the same as the ones they sewed from morning till night every day in the Grey House.

'Look,' said the soldier, opening the sack. It was full of letters. 'I put them in here.'

That prickly feeling was there . . . and then it disappeared.

The soldier popped both letters in and carefully pulled the string to close the sack.

'And that's it?'

'That's it.'

'They'll go into his hands personally?'

'Into his hands personally.'

'Thank you, Comrade Commander!' Shura shouted jubilantly.

The soldier nodded, then pushed the sack inside the door, which promptly closed, and he turned and walked away. The crowd parted timidly to make way for him. He was holding a folder under his arm. On the other side of the street, a black car was waiting for him.

Shura threw a victorious glance at the line. *The poor devils! You're only afraid if you're guilty. But everything's different if you've nothing to hide.*

A black car flew by with a snort. It puffed out that lovely smoky smell.

'Excuse me,' Shura exclaimed impatiently, pushing his way out of the crowd. He had no business with these people now.

They also made way for him to get out. In the distance, he could see the woman with the basket standing on the pavement. Shura waved to her, as if to say, *Everything's all right*.

The woman was impatient to hear the details and she ran out into the road.

'Hey!' Shura screamed.

He froze; a truck had turned the corner and was heading straight towards her. 'Get off the road!' he shouted.

He squeezed his eyes shut. He put his hands over his ears, aware that it wouldn't block out the awful sounds: the toot of a horn, the startled shriek, the crash of broken glass, the screams of passers-by, the policeman's whistle.

But he didn't hear any of that.

He dropped his hands. He opened his eyes. The woman

with the basket was hurrying over to him. The truck had missed her by some incomprehensible miracle.

'Why did you yell? What road?' said the woman as she approached.

Shura gulped. *What just happened?*

She handed him his cap back. 'Did you deliver the letters?'

Shura nodded.

'Really?' the woman asked suspiciously. 'You don't seem too pleased. How did it go?'

But that truck just ran straight through her! No, it can't have. I must have imagined it.

'It was all absolutely fine!' he said proudly, trying not to show his confusion. He pulled on his cap, then nudged it to the back of his head. 'Now they'll definitely let Mama and Papa out! And your husband, too,' he was quick to add.

The woman looked at the Raven's House with a combination of doubt and hope. 'When?'

Shura also turned to look at the building. He remembered the full sack. Shura imagined a gallant soldier carrying it off. So many letters! And they all needed to be read and acted upon. Shura did a rough calculation: the Raven's House had six floors; it was a wide building and went back a long way; and all the windows had lights on, people working away. Shura laughed.

'By the end of the day!' he announced confidently.

'He said that?'

'Of course,' Shura lied. He believed himself, as if he really had heard it from the soldier.

The woman looked at him incredulously. And Shura told her about the sack.

. . .

'Can you imagine, Tanya, what an idiot I was!' he groaned.

'You didn't know,' replied Tanya.

'Of course I did. I saw it. But it didn't make any sense.'

'Don't worry,' Tanya reassured him. 'Carry on.'

And Shura carried on telling her all about it.

. . .

'Are you hungry?' the woman asked.

Shura nodded. He was suddenly aware of his hunger. He also felt a tickle below his belly: he needed to go to the toilet. His legs were numb from standing.

'Let's go to my place. It's not far. We can stay there until the end of the day. Or is someone waiting for you? Where do you live?'

'It's OK. I can come to yours.'

Off they went. Shura was so pleased with himself that he didn't object when the woman led him by the hand like a little boy. *She probably doesn't have any children of her own, so all children seem little to her. Well, never mind,* thought Shura.

Everyone on the street seemed friendly. Even the dull, cloudy sky didn't spoil their mood.

The woman charged ahead, as if she wasn't going to give way to anyone. *A person can really change when they* think *they're right,* Shura thought.

They turned on to a large street. Trams and trucks all hurtled along. Occasionally a horse would trot past, pulling a cart, its hooves clicking.

Shura looked around cheerfully. The street reminded him of Liteiny Prospekt. The signboards, the arched gateways, the cast-iron posts holding up the tram wires overhead. The traffic lights flashed. Pedestrians were walking on the pavements in both directions.

It occurred to Shura now that everyone seemed to resemble a bird somehow. This man walking by was like a goose, with his skinny neck and a long nose. And those two there were like self-important grey hooded crows, strutting along, their hands behind their backs, looking contemptuously at those who were different. A turkey-woman passed by with heavy red earrings and a large drooping nose. A group of women hopped like sparrows from one shop to another, tweeting and chirping away. A woman with a rotund belly walked straight towards Shura. Her lips were pursed shut. She had small beady eyes. She minced along with short legs in short boots. The spitting image of a pigeon! Shura twisted his whole body to the side to avoid bumping into her.

'Why are you wriggling like that?' his new acquaintance asked, perplexed.

'No reason,' answered Shura. He stopped; the traffic light was red.

'My name is Elena,' she said, but she didn't stop at the crossing, and pulled Shura with her into the road. 'You can call me Elena Nikolaevna. Or Auntie Lena. Or just call me Lena. As you wish. And you?'

'Aaagh!' gasped Shura in horror as he saw the oncoming traffic picking up speed.

'What's wrong?' Lena asked casually.

Shura squirmed like a dog on a leash trying to pull her back on to the pavement. But Lena held his hand tightly.

'What's wrong with you?' she asked, oblivious to the traffic.

A truck's large-eyed snout was heading straight for them. *That's it — we're done for*, thought Shura. He didn't even have time to close his eyes. He saw clearly how the truck passed right through him: first the copper innards of the engine, then the weary driver in a shirt with buttons and a cigarette in the corner of his mouth, then the cages full of sleepy, fluffy chickens, piled one on top of another.

It didn't hurt; it didn't even tickle. It was as though nothing had happened.

'I asked, what's your name?' Lena tugged his hand. 'Can you hear me?'

'D-d-d . . .' Shura could not utter a word.

'Dima?' She stopped in the middle of the road.

'D-d-d-d . . .' He struggled to come to his senses.

'Daniel? David?'

'D-d-did you see that?' Shura finally managed to say. 'Look where you're going!' he squealed.

He shoved Lena on to the pavement. Just in time. But the second he did he felt someone walk right through him, looking straight ahead, strangely prickly with all her little worries. She looked like a magpie.

What? Am I invisible? Shura was stunned. He spread out his fingers and held his hand right up to his eyes. It looked like a normal hand. He couldn't see through it.

'Why did you push me?' asked Lena.

'Sorry. I didn't mean to,' said Shura. What else could he say?

She shifted the basket to her other hand. She gripped Shura's hand even tighter.

'Well, we're here now.'

Before them stood a pastel-pink tenement block decorated with swirly patterns, like so many apartment buildings in Leningrad. They walked through the archway.

Lena's room was warm and cosy. A soft grey light came in through the blinds. A neatly ironed shirt and a pair of trousers were laid out on the bed. A jacket hung on a hanger. It was as if their owner had popped out, but was due back any minute.

On a table in the middle of the room was a woollen blanket, wrapped up into a plump bundle. It was just like Shura's mama always did when she made them some hot stew or soup – she would wrap it up, to keep it warm for them to eat while she was at work.

'Do you have children?' Shura asked Lena.

She laughed. 'Children? Oh, no. We still need to finish university first. Get our degrees.'

Shura realized that she wasn't very old, still a student. Maybe he was the same with grown-ups as Lena was about children: she couldn't tell how old children were; and, to him, people were just either grown-ups or children. He couldn't easily tell how old an adult was by looking at them.

Lena kicked off her shoes. She unwound the blanket to reveal the pan.

'I always leave something for my husband when I'm not at home. In case he suddenly comes back while I'm out. He might be released at any moment. He isn't guilty of anything.'

As Lena began to warm up and thaw out, she started chatting incessantly. She ran to the kitchen and brought in a steaming kettle. She pulled several jars and packages out of her basket and placed them on the table.

'I took these for my husband. But it turned out they weren't needed. Why would he need them? He'll be let out later. It's a weight off my shoulders, really! He'll be released this evening. Maybe even earlier. Imagine: we're sitting here drinking tea – then the doorbell rings, and it's him. They'll explain everything and send him home. Eat, won't you!' Lena chattered away. 'I'll cook him a hot dinner this evening! Don't be shy. Help yourself to bread. Jam. Butter. Cheese. Sausage.'

Shura made a jam sandwich and bit into it. Never before had food tasted so good. After the grey mush he'd had to eat at the Grey House, everything seemed unbelievably delicious. The jam tasted like a rainbow on his tongue!

After lunch, Lena made space for him to nap on the slippery and creaky leather couch.

But Shura didn't manage to sleep. He had barely closed his eyes when Lena was shaking him by the shoulder.

'It's time to go! It's nearly the end of the working day.'

He came round with a jolt and sat up.

Lena was pulling on her coat, trying to get her arms into the sleeves. Finally, she got there. Shura didn't need to be told twice that it was time to go.

They went out into the street.

The sky was still as gloomy and dull as it had been that

morning, as if the day hadn't had the strength to get going and had skipped straight from dawn to dusk. Were it not for the clock on the cast-iron pole in the street, he might have concluded that time hadn't moved. Or perhaps time really had stood still, but the sharp black hand kept on ticking regardless, jumping from one marker to the next.

Shura and Lena walked quickly, as though their hurried pace would hasten the hour when office clerks would tidy away their papers and turn off their green lamps, and in the shops, they would start clearing the goods from the counter. The hour when Mama and Papa would walk out of the Raven's House holding hands and call out, 'Shura! What a good boy you are!' and the soldier in the blue cap would salute, apologizing for the mistake.

Pedestrians walked by without a glance and passed right through Shura and Lena. Lena didn't seem to notice. She was more concerned about the puddles on the pavement, carefully walking around them or hopping over.

So, we still need to avoid puddles, Shura told himself, trying to make sense of how it all worked. Sadly, he was only in the first class so he hadn't learnt about physics and chemistry yet. All he had done at school was animals and trees, just the basics so far, so he didn't know much about how these things worked. But Papa would know all about it, of course!

As they walked, Shura silently made a mental note of everything, so he could ask Papa about it later. He even started deliberately standing in people's way to see what it felt like.

He quickly amassed an entire collection:

- *a horse and cart: feels like someone's pulling a thread of yarn through you, and the horse leaves a warm feeling in your hands and feet for a while*
- *a whole kindergarten of little children walking in pairs, with two teachers, one up ahead and one behind: extremely tickly*
- *a lady in a beret: smelt nice*
- *a man in a cap: rough and scratchy*
- *a policeman: a slight metallic aftertaste on one side*
- *a truck labelled 'Fish': a pleasant chilly sensation inside*

Best of all was walking though the tram with the driver in his black cap, the noisy conductor and the tired, gloomy passengers. While the tram passed through him, Shura felt like he could read each passenger like a book, from cover to cover.

'Why are you jumping about all over the place?' asked Lena, taking his hand.

She had, apparently, got used to all these miracles and never seemed alarmed or excited or surprised. Or maybe her husband was all she thought about.

Once he had got used to this strange new way of walking, Shura found he had a bounce in his step. He enjoyed walking through Leningrad again after all this time, soaking up the musical chaos of the big city. Soon he would be back home, with Mama and Papa, Bobka and Tanya.

Now even the Raven's House seemed beautiful: all covered in orange squares of light against the background of the darkening sky.

There was no longer any queue. There was no one there at all. The hatch was closed.

'We're late!' Lena was horrified. 'It can't be.'

She blinked in fright, her eyelids flushed.

'Don't cry. Let's wait and see,' Shura said.

'It's all locked up.' Her voice quivered with tears.

'Wait a minute. Stay here!' Shura shouted to her.

So what if the door was locked? All you had to do was climb over the fence, crawl under the front gates, climb on to the shed or bend back a loose board on the back gate. There were so many different ways to sneak into a yard that only children knew.

'Uncle, what time is it?' Shura called out to a soldier who was crossing the road. He was wearing the same cap with the blue band, which meant he was heading to the Raven's House.

The soldier didn't respond. He didn't even see Shura.

All the better, Shura rejoiced. He followed the soldier, keeping close behind him. Just to check, he tried prodding him in the back. His hand went right through and the soldier didn't even twitch.

The soldier walked towards the arched entrance in the main wall that led through to the inner courtyard. As he approached, the gates began to open slowly. Shura sneaked in after him without stopping to think.

Inside was a tarmac-covered courtyard. There was a row of black cars and vans, all staring straight ahead with their identical, round headlights. Shura darted over to a car and pressed himself against its shiny, polished side, just in case. The soldier hadn't seen him and neither had the passers-by on the street. And yet Lena could. Until he figured out how this worked, it was better to be careful.

Shura peeped out from beside the van.

From the inner courtyard, the Raven's House loomed tall on all sides. In the centre of the courtyard, there was a strange little grey house with a small window on the side and a wide, semicircular door. There was a heap of sacks against the wall.

Another soldier came out of the Raven's House into the courtyard. He wasn't wearing a cap, but had a greatcoat draped over his shoulders. Shura could see the blue tabs on his collar.

He opened the window on the side of the little grey building. He started lighting matches and tossing them inside. He used the last match to light a cigarette. Puffing out blue smoke, he opened the door: inside everything was a blazing orange.

Oh! It's not a little house! It's a huge oven!

The soldier waited for the fire to get going. When he finished his cigarette, he threw the stub into the furnace. He took off his greatcoat, carefully draped it over the bonnet of a car, and straightened out his uniform. He picked up a sack. Then another and another. As he reached for the fourth sack, another slipped and fell from the heap. The soldier cursed. The sack burst open on one side and some letters spilled out with a rustle.

Eagle-eyed Shura managed to read the front of one: '*Comrade Raven – into his hands personally!*' The word 'personally' was underlined three times. Shura's heart skipped a beat. Was it someone asking for something? Or complaining?

They're bad people, criminals, he heard Papa's voice in his head.

168

The soldier grabbed the envelope, then started to pick up the rest. Some envelopes were thin, others were thick. The soldier flung them all into the oven. He scrunched up an almost-empty sack and hurled that in, too. Then he prodded the fire with the poker. Black smoke was rising from the chimney. The soldier went back to shifting sacks, dragging them closer to the fire-breathing mouth. Sack by sack, he fed the hungry beast.

Shura pressed himself closer to the side of the car.

Somewhere a door slammed. Another soldier came and joined the first one, his boots clicking on the tarmac.

'So, Misha, calling it a day?'

'Yeah, about time.'

'And my shift's just starting.' They both lit up cigarettes, exhaling blue-grey smoke and staring dreamily at the flames; the paper burned quickly.

Misha! thought Shura. *His name's Misha! Just Misha. They have the most ordinary names!* To Shura, that made what they were doing all the more shocking.

Suddenly a burning leaf of paper flew out of the furnace like a howl of despair. The soldier stabbed it with the poker and stamped on it with his boot.

'They keep scribbling away, these spies,' he said between puffs on his cigarette.

'They're scum!'

'Fed up?'

'So-so.'

'I'm not surprised, if you've read this stuff . . .' the first one said, sympathizing.

'Read them? These enemies all write the same drivel. Why bother reading it? Straight in the fire!'

Shura winced as though he meant Shura when he said: 'Straight in the fire!'

The second soldier slapped the first on the shoulder and left. The first soldier hurled the last sack into the oven and closed the door.

Shura's face was burning.

Behind him, the gates creaked open. A black car rumbled into the courtyard. The doors slammed shut after two soldiers got out, leading a man with his hands tied behind his back. They pushed him into the Raven's House.

Shura shuddered.

What now? Go back to the Grey House, the rattling sewing machines, Bollard . . .? No.

The gates released the black car back out on to the street. Night was hunting time. The gates slowly crept back towards each other.

Shura made a run for it. He slipped side on through the closing gates. Nipping the hem of his coat, the gate snapped shut behind him. He just made it.

Lena gave him a cheerful wave. Shura walked over to her on wobbly legs. He wished the ground would open and swallow him up. Lena's eyes twinkled with joy, as if she wanted to light up Shura's path.

Shura stopped. He lowered his gaze.

Lena ran up and put her arms around him. She gave him a big hug. She was laughing. No, crying. No, she was laughing with tears in her eyes.

'Thank you! Thank you!' she said, smothering Shura's cheeks with kisses. He didn't understand and just stared at her. 'There, at the hatch. I just knocked. Just like that. Without thinking. Suddenly there was a man – in uniform, in a blue cap. He heard me out, he didn't send me away. He replied! An answer to my letter!'

'It can't be!' shouted Shura. 'I've just . . .'

But she wasn't listening. 'Ten years, he said. He said, wait. My husband will be back in ten years. Only I mustn't write to him and I mustn't send telegrams.'

Shura looked at her with horror: ten years! He was seven.

'It's nothing. Ten years for love – it's nothing.' She was ecstatic.

Shura wanted to explain that they had lied to her. That they didn't read the letters. That they burned them all. That everything anyone wrote – the bags and bags and bags of letters – just went straight in the fire . . . That it wasn't a mistake. It was all true. Spies. Enemies. His lips began to quiver.

'What's wrong, little one? It's wonderful, isn't it? Hurrah!' She kissed him again. 'It means everything is OK!' She pulled her coat tightly around herself. 'Pop by and see me, if you ever need anything!' Lena patted him on the head and clumsily ran off.

Shura watched her as she got further away. Although Lena had invited him to hers in a cheerful voice, he realized that 'if you ever need anything' wasn't the same as 'right now'.

He shoved his hands into his pockets and set off walking. He turned on to the main street. Pedestrians flowed past. Cars rumbled past. At the crossroads, a policeman was doing a merry dance, his hands gesturing to the drivers whose turn it was to wait and whose to go.

The sky turned to night. Mandarin-orange light poured out from the windows. There were noticeably more people on the street. It was the hour when everyone set off for somewhere: to see friends, to the theatre or to the cinema. The early-evening hour that was especially pleasant for those who had someone waiting at home, even if it was only a cat, a dog or just a pot of hot tea – and that was especially lonely for those who had nowhere to go.

Shura wanted to get to Auntie Vera's as quickly as possible.

'Excuse me, which street is this?' asked Shura.

No one answered.

'Excuse me, how do I get to the Peter and Paul Fortress?'

Nobody even glanced in his direction.

'Hey, comrades, hello!'

Grey passers-by streamed shakily through Shura. The stocky duck-girls waddled, the pigeon-ladies minced along, the crows strutted about in their grey cloaks, the sparrow-shoppers bustled past, the magpies chattered and laughed. None of them saw him nor heard him.

'Comrades!' Shura shouted. 'Dear citizens, someone please . . .'

He stood in the middle of the pavement. Everyone walked right through him. They talked and laughed. Some scurried along, their noses down, shoulders raised. Some ambled by, hand in hand, others strode purposefully, with elbows out. Some shuffled their feet, while others hopped along, heels clicking.

Life rushed past Shura. The good, stable life he once knew. And, from what he could tell, there wasn't any room for him.

But did that mean that he, Shura, was guilty? Did it mean he was an enemy of the state and a spy?

'Hey, you!' In a sudden rage, Shura shoved a passing woman in a beret. But it was in vain: his hands went right through, and he flew headlong on to the pavement, not hitting anyone but himself. Nobody rushed to help him. No one noticed him. He sat on the ground and cried.

'You monsters!'

Shura sobbed for a moment, then he stood up. Lying on the ground beside him was a heap of cobblestones. There was a gaping hole in the pavement a bit further along. It looked as though the workers had been doing a giant jigsaw puzzle all day but had given up and gone home. He wiped his face with his sleeve. He picked up some stones in both hands and pressed them against his stomach.

'Well, just you wait, you beasts,' muttered Shura. His voice trembled with tears, resentment and fury. 'Now you'll notice me. Now I'll show you.'

He threw a stone at another woman in a little beret. Then a fat man with a briefcase, and a student, his jacket unbuttoned. But they all walked on, utterly oblivious. The stones flew right through them.

People kept walking by. Shura ran back to the heap of cobblestones for more. His tears were gone.

Shura was delirious, ecstatic at realizing that he could do whatever he liked. He picked up another handful. He spotted a target in the crowd. A boy. Hands in pockets. Button nose.

Cap pushed to the back of his head, a dirty scarf wrapped around his neck. A grubby shirt was showing under a jacket that didn't fit, that looked like it belonged to someone else. And he had odd boots on his feet: one black and newer, the other green with scuffed toes.

A ruffian! That was what the local district policeman called boys like that as he stalked around with his torch, chasing them out of basements and attics.

Shura took aim and threw a piece of cobble.

'Ow!' The boy looked up in surprise and rubbed his grubby forehead. 'Oi, you stinker!'

Shura's eyes burst open. The ruffian could see him! And now, with a confident swagger, the boy was heading straight for him!

On any other day Shura would have turned on his heels and fled. But now he was glad even to get into a fight, to have any kind of human contact.

The little ruffian strutted over. He glared at Shura and eyed him up and down. He had blue eyes, greasy hair. Filthy clothes. He stank of tarmac and another disgusting smell that reminded Shura of certain grown-ups.

The ruffian gnashed his teeth. He had several gaping holes where his teeth should have been. Shura clenched his fists and did a quick reckoning: they were almost the same height, though his opponent was slightly taller. Should he throw the first punch? Or wait? Shura's legs tensed.

At that moment a tall, handsome man – a sailor with a dagger in his belt – passed through the ruffian, as if through thin air. He was walking arm in arm with a girl, who was carrying a bouquet.

The puffed-up ruffian seemed to deflate. He jerked his chin out and glowered at them as they walked away. He growled. He snorted. He spat at them, but he didn't hit his target.

Shura relaxed his fists. Another invisible boy! It can't be. And yet – he could see Shura, so he must be the same. Or else how . . .?

'Who are you?' shouted Shura.

'And who are you?' the ruffian asked back.

'Shura.'

The boy swung his arm. *Now I'm going to get it*, Shura thought. But, instead of a punch, he gave Shura such a friendly slap on the shoulder that he was left reeling.

The boy solemnly announced: 'I'm the King of the Street.'

CHAPTER NINE

The first thing the King showed him was how to come by something to eat.

'You mean, steal it?'

At first, the King looked at Shura blankly. But then, when he understood, he burst out laughing.

'Yes, baby,' he said, patting Shura's head, although they were almost the same height. 'How have you only just cottoned on?'

Shura couldn't bear his condescending tone. But he felt embarrassed all the same.

'You can't take someone else's things,' said Shura, somewhat unsure of himself.

They stood at the entrance to a grocery shop. There were wooden blocks in the window, painted yellow to represent cheese and butter. And, although they didn't really look much like butter or cheese, the sight still made Shura's stomach growl. He was famished.

'Ah, forgive me, Your Highness,' said the King, doing an exaggerated bow. 'Please wait while I prepare a three-course dinner for Your Majesty.'

Shura didn't move.

The King stopped clowning around. 'It's easy. They can't see us.'

'So?'

'To hell with them.'

Shura peered into the shop, still feeling doubtful. He stepped back. *No*.

'Look!' cried the King. A pastry vendor trundled past with her cart, a thick blanket laid over the top. With a deft hand, the King lifted the edge of the blanket and whipped out a *pirozhok*. The vendor didn't bat an eyelid.

'Just like that,' he said, taking a bite.

The King chewed quickly. Shura imagined with horror how passers-by would now see this lump of food suspended in mid-air, being chewed and gradually sliding down an invisible gullet. There'd be panic, screams.

But nothing happened. The King popped the last piece in his mouth and wiped his fingers on his jacket.

'You see?' he said with his mouth full. 'I'll wait here for you.'

His legs trembling, Shura tiptoed into the shop. On the counter were yellow bars of butter. There were three or four women waiting in the queue. The grocer cut off chunks of butter with a long narrow knife that looked like a ruler and carefully placed the cubes on to brown paper with the tip of the knife. Then he carried the package to the scales, and everyone in the shop stared, hypnotized, at the hand on the dial as it wobbled before settling.

Shura approached gingerly from the side. The grocer cut off another small cube from the bar to round up the weight.

Shura quickly grabbed the chunk, threw it into his mouth and leapt back into the street.

The King stood by, watching. He had a newspaper under his arm, which he had apparently managed to pilfer while Shura was in the shop. While he was *stealing* from the shop. Shura's ears burned with shame. He sucked the piece of butter in his mouth, trying to swallow it as quickly as he could.

No one came out to chase him. Through the shop window, where thick wooden cartwheels were decorated with yellow blocks pretending to be cheese and butter, Shura saw the confused salesman staring at the bar of butter in front of him and searching for the vanished piece. He looked everywhere, even under the counter.

No one on the street yelled at Shura, either. No one stopped to stare and point at a piece of butter floating in the air and gradually melting. Pedestrians kept on walking by, staring straight ahead.

It was as though the chunk of butter had disappeared from one world and arrived in another. *Just like in the movies*, Shura thought. Surely physics had an explanation. But the King probably didn't know much about that either.

'Come on,' he said cheerfully.

In another shop, Shura was able to sneak a piece of smoked sausage just as easily. In a bakery, he helped himself to a delicious jam bun sprinkled with sugar. He promised himself that when Mama and Papa returned he would ask for some money the very next day, so he could go back to all the shops and pay for everything he had eaten.

Standing in the middle of the pavement, Shura nibbled at the bun. Under the light of the street lamps, passers-by were hurrying about their business, swinging their briefcases as they walked. Trams clattered by, full of passengers, sometimes spraying out sparks. Black Ford motorcars rumbled by.

The King deftly swiped a packet of cigarettes from a street vendor's tray. He popped one in his mouth.

'What are you doing?' spluttered Shura, his mouth full.

The King pulled some matches out of a pocket. He struck one and lit a cigarette. He took a couple of puffs, holding the blue-grey smoke in his cheeks before blowing it out through his pursed lips. Only then did he reply. 'What?' He held out the packet. 'Want one?'

'Children don't smoke.'

'Children play with toys,' the King replied in a mocking tone. 'Balls and stuff. Have you got a ball? Is someone going to tuck you into bed tonight? Are you going to school tomorrow?' And again he held the packet out to Shura. 'You sure?'

Shura refused the offer with a shake of his head.

The King wasn't offended. 'Don't worry. You'll learn.' He finished the cigarette he was holding with two grubby fingers, then stubbed it out on the sole of his shoe.

'Bedtime.' The King took the newspaper from under his arm and waved it like a conductor's baton. 'Let's go and make ourselves at home.'

Shura knew that boys like the King were not welcome anywhere. Wherever they went, they were shouted at by caretakers who chased them away with their brooms, and policemen blew their whistles and shook their fists at them. But the King didn't care. Shura envied him.

They sneaked into several houses through the front door and crept upstairs to the top floor, to see if the door to the attic was open. Finally, they found one that wasn't locked. The King divided the newspaper up into sheets and made something resembling a nest. One for himself. And one for Shura.

'Thank you!'

'Hey, don't get any ideas. You'd best learn yourself. You're making your own next time.'

Shura carefully positioned himself under the newspaper sheets. Shura was impressed at how well the paper held the heat. He couldn't help but say so: 'Amazing!'

The King laughed. 'I know I am,' he said majestically.

The next morning Shura opened his eyes and the first thing he saw was the King. He was holding a small, rectangular card. Shura checked his cap. The photograph!

'Hey! Give it back!'

'Who is it?' asked the King. 'What a hat! Ooh la la.' But he was staring at it longingly.

Shura tried to snatch the photograph back. The King grabbed his arm.

'Get lost!'

'Give it back!'

'All right, all right, I'm not going to eat it. Just having a look.' He gazed at the photograph for a long time, as if it reminded him of something important, something precious. He turned it over. On the back were some slanting lines of

180

writing. The ink was smudged in places. Shura saw that the King was looking at it upside down. He obviously couldn't read. He looked at the picture again.

'Is it your mam? Gran?'

'I don't know who it is.'

'You're lying.'

'I don't know her.'

'Aha, you stole it.'

'Give it back!'

'She looks like one of our lot.' The King handed the card back.

'One of who?' Shura stuffed it back into his cap.

'Come on,' the King shrugged, avoiding the question. 'Time for some scoff. That was a long sleep – I'm starving.'

They headed to the bakery for their morning forage. There was a queue of women in front of the counter. Shura and the King carefully studied the pyramid-shaped mounds of bread rolls and loaves. Behind the saleswoman hung ring-shaped *bubliks*, threaded together on string. The smell of the bread made Shura dizzy.

The King followed his nose as he considered what to have for breakfast.

'Uh-oh,' said Shura, grabbing him by the sleeve.

'Hey! What?' The King wasn't pleased about being distracted.

'Look,' Shura pointed.

A woman was staring at them. She was holding a string shopping bag.

'Ah, don't worry. She's not after us. She's looking at

something behind us,' the King reassured him. And he walked back over to the rolls.

The woman kept on staring, her eyes wide. Shura couldn't look away. She was definitely staring straight at them!

'King,' he whispered.

But the King just waved it off. He grabbed a roll.

'Police!' shouted a woman, leaping after them. But no one in the queue turned to look. Shura and the King tumbled out on to the street. They ran and ran, blown by the wind along the busy street. Eventually they stopped.

'Did you see that? What happened?' Shura exclaimed breathlessly.

The King frowned and pulled out his cigarettes.

'Strange,' he muttered, a cigarette between his lips as he struck a match.

Shura had never seen him break into a sweat like that before.

'She could see us!' exclaimed Shura.

The match broke. The King threw it away and shoved the cigarettes back in his pocket.

'That means she was invisible, too,' realized the King.

Of course, thought Shura. *No one reacted when she shouted. Nobody even turned round.* He remembered how the truck drove right through Lena and kept on going.

'It's just that she hasn't realized,' the King continued to reason. 'She hasn't worked it out yet.'

Shura remembered the queue outside the Raven's House. *Those people* could see him, so they must have been invisible, too. There were hundreds of them queuing through the night.

But they wouldn't be standing there waiting forever. They must be walking around the city, waiting for the tram, amid the crowds on the street and in the squares. But who would notice a few hundred or even thousand in a city as large as Leningrad? In a country as large as the Soviet Union?

Shura wondered if he should tell the King about the people in the queue. But instead he asked, 'Why can't they see us?'

Shura and the King weren't transparent in the slightest. They were normal people. They got hungry and they ate, they needed the toilet, they slept, they felt cold and tired like everybody else.

The King snorted. 'They don't want to see us, so they don't.'

'Is that really possible?' Shura was amazed.

'Well, it's how it is,' said the King. He sucked in the air through a gap in his teeth.

After that they continued to come across invisible people. Shura was no longer surprised by it. But what continued to confuse him was when he saw invisible people shying away from others who were the same.

Then he started to realize. They must have all been struck at some point by the same horrible events as Shura. This same thing had happened to them, which made everyone else turn against them and refuse to talk to them, or even see or hear them – and yet some of these invisible people refused to accept their fate. They acted as though they were normal, because they were trying with all their strength to hide what had happened to them.

They did what they could to carry on with their ordinary lives, pretending that nothing had happened. For some it worked. They carried on doing their jobs. They carried on living in the same room as before. They even became a little less invisible because of the way they tried to fit in, and other people said hello to them and shook their hands, and they were invited to events and meetings as before.

They were afraid of losing that connection to normal life, so they turned away and refused to speak to others who had suffered the same fate. They avoided eye contact and refused to see them or hear them. They didn't notice when Shura passed through them.

But not everyone was like that, fortunately. Once a woman in an apron chased them at the market. They had tried, and failed, to steal a sausage.

The King flew ahead. The woman caught up with Shura, shoved him in the back and knocked him to the ground. *She's going to kill me*, he thought. But instead she handed him a sausage. Then she trudged back to her counter. The only reason she chased them was because she was pretending to be an ordinary person!

Shura and the King tore the sausage in half to share.

'That was strange.'

'Yeah, strange,' agreed the King, chewing. He swallowed his mouthful and added, 'We need to switch locations more often. If we stand out, we'll get caught.'

The King of the Street knew everything. Where was the best spot to steal a big warm jam bun? The answer: everywhere, but, best of all, at the bakery on the corner, early in the morning when the truck labelled 'BREAD' backed up to the window of the bakery, and the driver, with his thick mitts on, noisily unloaded the flat wide crates of delicious-smelling buns and steaming-hot bread.

Where was the best place to sit during the day and hide from the cold? The answer: among the thick warm pipes in the basements and attics. Where was the best place to sleep? Here there wasn't just one answer. Most of all, Shura liked to sleep in a huge cooking pot. There were massive black cauldrons where workers melted the buttery tarmac to smear on the roads. Then at the end of the day they put the fire out and went home. But these large cauldrons stayed toasty and warm all night.

The King had a distinct knack for finding the streets where they were repairing the road surface. By smell, perhaps? At first, Shura couldn't sleep because of the sharp, resinous odour of the tarmac. Then with time he got used to it. He shifted his cap to his face and stuck his hands under his armpits. He snuggled up, cosily embraced by the warm walls of the cauldron around him. The King would sleep alongside him. Sometimes in the middle of the night a stray cat would gently jump down on to them, searching for a night's lodging in the same place. But, realizing its mistake, it would quickly scamper away.

In the early days, Shura still tried to find Auntie Vera's flat. But the King didn't know what the streets were called. He had never heard of the Peter and Paul Fortress.

'And the Hermitage?' asked Shura. 'And the Russian Museum? What about the zoo?'

'No such thing here,' said the King, shrugging his shoulders.

'Here? Isn't this Leningrad?' Shura was surprised.

'Yeah. It's just the other side.'

Shura didn't understand. The King got impatient and called him a dunce, but he couldn't explain what he meant.

But, besides, how would Auntie Vera react when Shura, the son of spies and enemies of the state, appeared on her doorstep? Would she be happy to see him?

The King didn't have a father. Or a mother. Or a brother or a sister. He didn't have a home. Never had. Or so he claimed.

'You must have,' insisted Shura. 'Everyone comes from somewhere!'

But the King simply shrugged. He lived day by day, step by step, thinking only of the next problem: where to eat, where to hide, where to sleep.

Gradually Shura also picked up the skills of the street. They stole food and tobacco. In the afternoons they would hang around the streets and go to the cinema. At night they hid in cellars, attics, tarmac cauldrons. The prowling cats, usually so haughty and independent, began to come to them at night, snuggling up next to them.

The nights grew colder. And they had already seen all the movies several times. Shura didn't ask what they would do in the winter. He was sure that the King had a plan up his sleeve. But Shura was wrong. In fact, he knew nothing about the King.

There was one time when the King was in an unusually dreamy mood. They had settled for the night in an attic, wrapped in their stolen newspapers like blankets. From somewhere in the distance they heard a sound: someone below was playing the piano. The melody rose up through the floorboards. For some time, the King listened in silence.

'We had a grand piano,' he said. 'In the dining room. And . . .'

'What? A piano at home? And a dining room? Impossible! You can't have a dining room in a flat!' Shura laughed.

'You can,' muttered the King.

'What! A dining room? Dining rooms are in schools. Or hospitals. You don't get a dining room in a flat!' Shura had only ever lived in their two rooms in a communal flat. Just like everyone he knew in Leningrad. 'What a silly thing to say!' said Shura, chuckling to himself.

The King laughed, too. But in a slightly unconvincing way. He never asked Shura about himself. Sometimes Shura started talking about the Grey House. The King laughed at the strange names. He didn't react when Shura mentioned the eyes and the ears in the wall.

Just once he asked, 'They gave you scoff every day? Three times a day?' His eyes twinkled with a secret thought. But Shura didn't pay much attention. And even if he had paid attention – so what? Shura didn't have any other friends in this strange *not*-Leningrad, this city that looked so like his home city, and yet felt so strange.

Winter started flexing its muscles before it really got going across the city. Puddles were occasionally frozen over in the morning. Soon after the first frosts, the shop windows were decorated with portraits of Stalin. Mostly, the portraits showed a large beaky nose and a black moustache; some had something distinctly raven-like about them.

Banners with slogans were hung across the fronts of houses. Hammers hammered away and the squares were filled with platforms and stages. Caretakers swept the streets with real gusto. Workers hung up fir garlands woven with ribbons. Everywhere they looked they saw banners reading 'HAPPY 7TH NOVEMBER' and 'DAY OF THE REVOLUTION'. Shura was surprised; even in this not-Leningrad, they still celebrated Soviet holidays.

Columns of Pioneers passed by, merrily beating their drums, their fists alternating up and down in time with the rhythm: left, right, left, right. Legs together, they marched as one. They were practising for the major parade through the main square.

'At ease!' shouted their leader. The children started messing around, the boys provoking the girls, the girls teasing the boys, all of them laughing, shouting, singing songs together.

Shura noticed the melancholy look on the King's face as he watched them.

'Come on! Let's go and sing with them a little,' suggested Shura. 'They can't see us anyway.'

The King's lips trembled at the words '*They can't see us*'. He grabbed a piece of brick and flung it at the Pioneers. The stone hurtled through the crowd and Shura was relieved that it didn't hit anyone. It rolled across the ground.

The Pioneers passed by. The air was filled with the rattle

and rumble of the drums, the sharp screech of the copper bugles, the children's laughter. The King watched them as they walked away.

'Let's go, King.' Shura tugged at his sleeve. 'To the market. Pinch some scoff. Sausages today? Some apples . . . Eh, it's not bad when they can't see you!' He spoke with exaggerated enthusiasm, trying to cheer his friend up.

The King turned away. He bit his lip. Shura felt sorry for him. The independent and irreverent King was lonely.

'Have it,' said Shura that evening. He held out the photograph. The lady in the hat. The corners of the photograph were creased and the card had got softer with time. The King looked at him with disbelief.

'What do you want for it?'

'Nothing. You can just have it.'

The King held out his grubby hand. He held the photograph carefully, so it didn't get dirty. It was dark in the basement. You could just make out the white of the flowers on the huge hat. The King took out a match and lit it. He wanted to properly admire his present. When the match burnt out he tossed it away, then lit another one.

'And what does it say here?' he said, turning the photograph over.

'What?' Shura was indignant. 'You can't read someone else's message!'

'But it's OK to nick it?'

Shura stopped short. He couldn't argue with that.

'Who did you pinch it from?'

Shura told him about Bollard. The King turned the picture over again. In the light of the match, Shura imagined for a moment that he saw a resemblance to Bollard. As if a monster had swallowed up this beautiful young lady and now she was trapped in that horrible body.

The light burnt out.

Or at least that's what Shura thought, but in fact a spark had lit in the King's mind.

'Read it to me,' the King pestered him the next day.

'You can't read someone else's letter,' Shura insisted. He had a stolen bottle of milk in his hand. The King looked at it with a raised eyebrow and chuckled. Shura blushed.

The King looked eagerly at the strange symbols he couldn't decipher.

'I don't want to read everything. I just want to know the name maybe. Perhaps there's an address.'

'Why?'

'What do you care? Never mind . . . pig,' he snapped, hiding away the photograph.

'You want me to make you Prince of the Street?' he asked on another occasion. 'This side'll be mine, and that'll be yours. Eh? Prince? What do you say?'

The next day he was still going on about it. 'Who taught you everything? Who showed you the tarmac cauldrons? Who saved you every time you were in trouble? You ungrateful pig.'

Shura flinched.

The King quickly pulled out the photograph.

Shura gave in. 'I'll just look at the name – but that's it!'

'OK, but take your fat hands off!' grumbled the King. 'Watch it! Don't get it dirty! You can read it while I hold it.'

Shura hovered over the card, craning his neck to decipher the writing. He stared hard at the wiggly script. They weren't the same kind of letters that he had learnt at school! The school ones were like typed print: strong, clear, angular, and each one standing on its own. But these ones were how grown-ups wrote. They were loopy and clumped together in groups. The only thing he could make out was where one word ended and the next began.

'Well?' The King jabbed Shura in the ribs. In frustration, he exclaimed: 'You're supposed to be able to read!'

He himself began to examine the lines of text. 'Look, this looks just like an address.' The King pointed a dirty fingernail to two numbers at the bottom: 8 and 4.

'It might be the year.'

'I think it's the house number,' the King said confidently.

Shura frowned as he stared at the scrawl. There was a pointy capital letter that looked a bit like an 'M'. The circle next to it could surely only be an 'o'?

'*Mo*–,' he read out.

'Morskaya? Marata?' guessed the King, suggesting the names of streets. 'Manège Square?'

'You wally! I said "o". Marata and Manège Square are spelled with an "a".'

The King didn't answer.

'Moyka?' he suggested after a pause.

Shura counted the letters after 'Mo'. There were three more. 'Could be,' he confirmed.

'Aha!' the King exclaimed, waving his fist triumphantly. 'See? I can work it out, too. I'm no worse at reading than you.' And he whisked away the photograph and tucked it inside his coat.

This was strange, Shura realized; when he had wanted to find his aunt, the King had insisted that he'd never heard of the Peter and Paul Fortress, or the zoo or the Hermitage. And now it turned out that he knew Moyka Street. And Morskaya Street, Marata Street and Manège Square.

But Shura shooed away the unpleasant, niggling feeling.

They hung around for a while on the streets, looking for something to steal for lunch. They wandered from shop to shop, from market to market. From one stall to another. The King didn't feel like anything today.

'Apples?' Shura suggested.

'Too sour.'

'A bread roll?'

'Sick of bread.'

'Ham?'

'I fancy fish.'

'Herrings?'

'Then we'll be thirsty later.' Stubbornly, the King dragged Shura on and on.

Then, finally, he exclaimed: 'Hurrah!'

'What?'

There weren't any shops at all where they were. They were walking along the River Moyka embankment and the only shop signs were further on: 'BATH HOUSE' and 'KEROSENE'. Through the cast-iron railings Shura saw the water splashing, the river's banks housed in granite.

Something didn't feel quite right.

'There's the house,' said the King, pointing a dirty finger. 'Number 84.'

The house was grey, with a touch here and there revealing how it had once been pastel pink. The plaster on the patterned front was chipped and peeling.

'Come on!' he said, pulling Shura by the sleeve.

'Are you crazy?'

'Why?'

'You want to go to Bollard?'

'Why Bollard?' the King answered with affected indifference.

'It's her photograph.'

'It's not of her.'

'How d'you know?'

The King chuckled. 'You said yourself Bollard's like a hippopotamus. Does it look like one in the picture?'

'I said rhinoceros . . . But so what?'

'She must've nicked it from somewhere. Like you.'

Shura blushed.

'Why would she steal someone else's photograph?'

'Well, why did you?'

Shura didn't have an answer.

'So, here we are: two kind boys, bringing it back. And as a reward, they'll pile our plates high with scoff.'

Shura had his doubts about this plan. But the King knew life – and his knowledge hadn't let them down so far.

'You scared?' the King asked arrogantly. 'Stay here, then. All the more for me.' He patted his belly. 'My tummy's rumbling.'

Reluctantly, Shura trailed after the King.

'And the flat number?' he shouted after the King.

The King brushed the question aside. 'Let's wait here. Maybe we'll recognize her. Her in the hat.' He pushed the front door. It was locked.

Shura was relieved. He didn't like this plan.

But the King wasn't going to back down. He stepped back from the house and had a look around.

'Let's go round to the yard.'

Their steps echoed loudly as they walked through the archway to the courtyard. A woman carrying a string shopping bag walked straight through them. She didn't bear any resemblance to the lady in the photograph.

In the courtyard, a bearded caretaker dressed in grey was sweeping the tarmac. Behind him was the grey-yellow of the building. The silhouette of the bare poplar trees stood out stark and black. A stripy cat trotted along near the wall. Another arch led through to the second courtyard.

The King boldly followed a course aiming directly for the caretaker's rectangular back. Caretakers usually chased away boys like him with a screech of their whistle, swiping at their legs with the broom. Being invisible certainly had its advantages.

The King turned to Shura, as if to say, *Look!* He stuck out his tongue – and crashed into the caretaker!

The man dropped his broom, and seized him with the swiftness of a tiger. Shura made a run for it. He sensed danger. The King pounded the air with his fists.

'Aagh!' shouted Shura, beating at the arm that suddenly grabbed him around the waist.

'Shut it!' the caretaker ordered through clenched teeth. 'Silence!' He shook them both like kittens.

There were a lot of books in the caretaker's room. Shura never imagined that a caretaker would read. The King cast a sidelong glance at the door.

'Sit still,' the man ordered, raising his finger in a threatening gesture. Shura and the King were at the table, sitting up straight.

An old woman appeared at the door. 'Oh my!' she gasped in surprise.

Shura and the King turned their heads. The caretaker and the old woman stood there frozen, staring at the wall. Something was sprouting from the wall. It stretched and unfurled like a burdock leaf. It was an ear.

The King jumped in his chair and Shura tensed up with fear.

The caretaker quietly went over to a cupboard and took out a radio set. He placed it beneath the ear and turned it on. As he twisted the knob, the ear strained anxiously towards the crackle emitted by the radio. Suddenly the music flowed, with violins and a piano melody floating by above the noisy ocean spray. The man turned the volume up. The ear twisted from side to side. But it couldn't pick up anything from further away than the wall.

The King stared wide-eyed at the ear. Shura realized that until then the King hadn't believed a single word he had said when he described the eyes and ears on the walls of the Grey House. Well, now he knew it was true.

'Now, speak,' said the caretaker. 'Where did you get this photo?'

The woman put her hands up to her cheeks. 'Oh my goodness!'

'Is it you?' Shura asked.

'No. What are you saying, boy? No! I don't even know who it is.' She turned the photograph over and smiled wistfully. 'Eighty-four. 1884. A whole eternity ago.'

Shura threw a scornful glance at the King. *House number? I told you it wasn't!*

The King answered with a sullen grimace.

'Let me see.' The caretaker put on his glasses. 'No, she doesn't live here. It must be someone's mother in her youth,' he suggested. He put the photograph aside.

Not just someone's mother, Shura realized. *It's Bollard's mother!* He was stunned by the realization that Bollard had a mother. Bollard had been a little girl! The photograph lay on the table, dirty against the gleaming white tablecloth.

'What's your story, boys? Tell me everything, from the beginning,' said the caretaker. He stood by the window, looking out at the grey courtyard. Shura kicked the King under the table, as if to say, *Help me out!*

'So, we're basically street kids,' the King began. He squinted at the ear. Exhausted by the continuous stream of music, it had drooped and slightly withdrawn into the wall.

Shura and the King, interrupting each other, told the story of how they had met. They told their story backwards, clearly starting at the wrong end. But no one minded.

The King paused cautiously. Shura hardly noticed that he was now talking on his own.

The man listened attentively. Then he walked over to the table. He squeezed the back of the chair so hard that his knuckles turned white. As soon as Shura mentioned the Raven's House, the caretaker crashed down on to the chair, which creaked under him. He covered his face with his hands. The old woman came over and put an arm around his shoulders. Heavy tears dripped soundlessly on to the tablecloth. The caretaker was crying!

This was their chance to make a run for it. No one would follow them now. But neither moved a muscle.

'Is that where you got the photograph?' the old woman asked.

Shura flinched. *Now she's going to lay into me*, he thought.

'No. There were only letters there. It's a huge building. With a courtyard in the middle. And in the yard there's a stove. And some black cars. And a man in a blue cap. Two men. They brought the sacks full of letters and shoved them into the furnace. One of the bags fell over and I saw the letters that spilled out. And then I ran away.'

'Feed them. They must be hungry,' the caretaker said in a dull voice from behind his hands.

'Are you hungry?' the old woman asked sympathetically.

Shura gulped, swallowing his saliva. The King nodded.

Shura's thoughts were rushing around his head as he tried

to make sense of all this. This couple could see them, which meant they also must be invisible, outsiders cut off from the world like Shura and the King. It seemed like outside in the yard, in public, they pretended to be normal and the caretaker carried on doing his job, but here, behind closed doors, they no longer pretended. They didn't look away to avoid making eye contact with Shura and the King. The caretaker hadn't tried to sneak past or keep out of their way.

The fact that the couple could see them and touch them must have meant that something awful had happened to them, just like Shura and the King. Just like Lena and all those invisible people Shura had seen and talked to in the queue at the Raven's House. But *why* were the caretaker and his wife invisible like them? Had someone in their family been taken away?

The old woman went out, carefully closing the door behind her. The man blew his nose noisily. And again he fell silent, looking at his hands as they lay on the table.

The King glanced at Shura and caught his eye, as if to say, *So, should we make a run for it?*

But then the old woman came back in. She nudged the door closed. She was holding a hot casserole dish, wrapped in a towel. From the pot rose grey-blue steam and the delicious aroma of meat stewed on the bone. It was difficult to think about anything else now.

Shura's stomach growled, bursting into life like an orchestra tuning up. But the old woman's movements were painfully slow as she laid the bowls out on the table. Slowly, slowly she laid out the spoons . . .

'Wash your hands,' said the caretaker, nodding towards the small enamel washbasin in the corner of the room. Beneath it, on the floor, was a stool with a washing-up bowl on it and a pink bar of soap.

When the King washed his hands, the water flowed black, and the soap lather turned grey-brown. He smeared traces of grey on the towel.

'Yours are no better,' said the King, as Shura began to lather his hands.

'Sit down, boys,' said the old woman.

The King immediately began shovelling in hot broth with the spoon, burning his mouth.

'My sister,' the caretaker said suddenly, his voice raw. 'She was arrested. Like your mother. And your father.'

Shura dropped the soap into the basin.

'By mistake?' he asked. Shura felt a great desire to say something positive. After all, they weren't to blame for the fact that the caretaker's sister had turned out to be a spy! It wasn't them who collected state secrets and gave them to their enemies. They didn't harm good Soviet people. 'Was your sister taken by mistake?'

The man thumped his palm so hard on the table that the spoons jumped. The King's soup splashed on to the tablecloth.

'It wasn't a mistake!'

The ear jerked into action.

The old woman walked up to the wall and gently plugged the ear hole with breadcrumbs.

'She wasn't guilty of anything,' said the caretaker. 'Neither was your mother! Or your father! It's not a mistake when they seize thousands of innocent people, thousands of honest people! Thousands! That's no mistake. They're seizing innocent people. And they do it knowingly!'

'My dear, please . . .' the old woman said reproachfully.

Shura stared at them with wide eyes, struggling to take in what he was hearing. The King quietly pulled the photograph across the table towards him. It disappeared into his pocket.

'We stood in that queue for so long to bring her food, warm clothes,' the old woman spoke softly.

Shura suddenly remembered their mama throwing woollen winter clothes into a suitcase.

The old woman shook her head. 'We stood there all night.'

'And the whole line was full of innocent people! Hundreds of them! Every day! Thousands! Do you understand? Nothing about it is a mistake!' The man was shouting in a choked voice.

'Hush now,' whispered the old woman, alarmed.

The King lowered his spoon. 'It's time for us to go,' he said, getting up from the table.

'No, no, boys! No, stay. Relax. Have a nap,' insisted the old woman, beginning to fuss over them.

But the King was already at the door. The old woman put a hand on his shoulder.

'Don't you dare touch me!' the King suddenly screamed.

The old woman recoiled. Shura tensed up in shock.

'Of course it's not a mistake!' the King shouted. 'It's all because of you lot! It's people like you who are to blame!'

'Boy! Please!'

'My papa and mama were against the Soviet people,' the

King yelled. 'They got arrested because they were selfish vermin! They never once asked me what I thought! Maybe I didn't want to live on the streets! I want to live in a house and go to school like everyone else! All this is because of them! Because of people like you! You vermin!' He turned and ran out of the room, down the corridor.

'Wait!' Shura shouted, rushing after him. They ran down the stairs and out through the yard. It was only out on the embankment that Shura managed to catch up with him.

'What was that about?'

'Push off! It's not their picture. That was obvious.'

'Where are you going?'

The King stopped. He moved the photograph into his inner pocket and pulled his jacket tightly around himself.

'Where do you think? To Bollard!' The King shrugged his shoulders.

Shura was speechless. *To Bollard?*

The King had nothing to hide. 'Would you rather see me freeze to death?'

'I thought you had a plan!'

'I do have a plan. We're going to go and hand ourselves in to the Grey House.'

Shura couldn't believe his ears. 'Hand ourselves in? To the Grey House? King, are you crazy?'

'Do you remember the way there? Let's go.'

'What?' Shura stood as if pinned to the spot. 'You planned this from the very beginning!' Shura realized. The King must have thought of it long ago and had been leading him on the whole time.

'You said yourself that they feed you and they have blankets. Everything is there, served up on a plate,' retorted the King angrily. He put his hands in his pockets. His face was impatient. 'Well, are you going to show me the way or not?'

He didn't get an answer.

'Well, then I'll find it myself. *Adieu!*'

'Wait!' Shura rushed after him. 'But you —'

'And I'm not going to scream their stupid slogans and drum along with them, in case you're wondering.'

'Then they'll —'

The King spat. Lazily he replied, 'We'll get fed there. We'll get clothes. We'll sit out the winter. And in spring we'll make a run for it.' The King stared at him with his bright blue eyes, waiting for an answer.

How could Shura make him understand that everyone who arrived at the Grey House ended up broken? That everyone fell under their control. It made no difference whether you were brave, kind, cheeky, strong-willed, shy, smart or quick-witted. *Everyone* was reduced to identical grey shadows. They walked in formation. They obeyed every command and worked their fingers to the bone. And the main thing . . .

But the King wasn't listening.

'I don't care,' he said. 'I don't need your help. I'll find it myself.'

He turned and walked away.

'Boy! Boy!' came a voice behind Shura. The old woman was hurrying towards him from the archway.

'What are you doing running off without your coat?' She handed Shura his coat and helped him into the sleeves. 'Where's your comrade?' But she understood even before Shura had a chance to reply. 'They'll come now because of his outburst,' she said. She looked at Shura.

He knew now who she meant by 'they'. The Raven's men, who had arrested his mother and father. Who had locked him up at the Grey House. Whose black cars prowled around the city, collecting victims. Black cars . . . on the prowl for prey like black ravens.

The old woman looked at the water. The waves splashed and slapped against the granite embankment wall.

Shura's stomach tightened. He knew she was going to send him away. He would be arrested, too, if he stayed here. But walking away now meant being alone again. Invisible on the grey streets that he could make no sense of.

Without a word, the old woman placed her hand on Shura's head. Her fingers tousled his hair. Then she embraced him tightly in her arms.

'Don't worry.'

Her coat was wet with tears.

'I brought him here,' said Shura, crying. 'I'm sorry.'

'They won't get here until evening,' said the caretaker, approaching them with the broom in his hand. Perched on his nose were his glasses with gold frames, which he had forgotten to take off. The glasses belonged to the room with the books and seemed at odds with his broom and apron. 'They only go around at night,' he reminded them.

Shura wiped his cheeks with his hand. 'Why not in the day?'

'They're afraid of daylight.'

'We need to run and tell everyone!' said Shura decisively. 'They're taking innocent people! That's what's happening!'

But the old man and woman paid no attention.

'I'm afraid for him,' the woman said to her husband, meaning Shura. They exchanged a glance, as though silently deliberating about what to do.

'Where does your aunt live?' the old woman asked Shura. He'd told them about his aunt at the table.

'On the other side of the bridge.' Shura's lip trembled again. Now she would ask for the address. He didn't know the name of the street or the number of the house. Why had he needed to know? After all, he used to have a papa and a mama. And Tanya. They knew.

'There are a lot of bridges in Leningrad,' said the old woman.

'Tuchkov Bridge?' The caretaker began listing names. 'Palace Bridge? Trinity? Liteiny? Hey! Are you listening? Okhtinsky?'

Shura just stood with his mouth gaping in surprise. 'Leningrad? You said Leningrad?'

The old woman looked puzzled.

'And there's a Hermitage here?' asked Shura excitedly, shaking her hand.

'Of course. But . . .'

'And a zoo?'

The old woman nodded. 'Yes, but . . .'

'And the Peter and Paul Fortress?' Bouncing ecstatically, with tears in his eyes, Shura grabbed them both by the hands.

Between him, the caretaker and his wife, the broom stood up straight like the fourth person in a round dance.

'Have you gone mad? Why are you hopping about?'

'Stop it! You're making me giddy.'

If this was the real Leningrad after all, that meant the King had lied to him. But why? Why had he pretended this was some other kind of city, some *not*-Leningrad? Was he afraid that he would lose Shura, and that he, the King, would again be left alone in the streets? Poor boy. Shura wasn't angry at him.

'That's the bridge!' he shouted with glee. 'The one near the Peter and Paul Fortress! My aunt lives near there.'

'Why didn't you just say so?'

'Why the tears?'

'Take the trolleybus,' the caretaker advised.

'We usually walk,' Shura replied. 'And then take the tram.'

'Good luck,' said the man. He shook Shura's hand and went back through the archway.

'He's not really a caretaker, is he?' asked Shura.

The old woman's anxious expression smoothed over. 'He was a scientist. A professor.'

'And what happened?' Shura for some reason thought about Bollard and the picture of the lady in the hat again. Perhaps they were mother and daughter. Maybe Bollard wasn't what she seemed?

But the old woman didn't have time to answer, because Shura suddenly groaned.

'Boy, what's wrong?'

Shura felt dizzy. His knees went limp. His stomach started churning.

'Are you feeling sick? Sit down!'

He crouched down and leant back against a granite post. The old woman fussed over him, doing all kinds of unnecessary things, trying to help. She straightened his collar and brushed off a speck of dust. She touched his forehead. 'I'll call my husband. Sit here.'

'No need,' Shura insisted, standing up straight again. Inside was a terrible weight.

'Are you sure you're not sick?'

Shura shook his head. He didn't dare admit how ill he felt.

'Come on.'

They walked a little.

'The King is kind. Don't think badly of him.'

'I know. He's been brainwashed. That's what they do.'

Shura tried to control his breathing. Something wasn't right inside.

'Are you feeling OK? You've gone quite green.'

'I'm fine,' he answered. Shura tried not to think about it. He would get to Auntie Vera's, and he could be ill there. But not right now. He didn't want to scare off the old woman – he needed her, he couldn't get there alone.

She seemed to believe Shura and started walking more quickly.

They reached a broad junction. The grey buildings frowned with their dark windows. Grey clouds hung low overhead.

'But why?' Shura asked. 'Why is the Raven doing all this?'

'The Raven?' said the old woman, puzzled by the mention. Her eyebrows jumped up in surprise. 'Raven?'

A piercing whistle shrilled through the air. The old woman stopped abruptly.

In the middle of the crossroads stood a policeman in a shiny helmet, whistle in his mouth. He spun round on the spot, signalling with his baton: *Attention!* And then: *Stop!*

The policeman stopped the traffic from all directions. Instead, the road filled with schoolchildren as they marched across, banging their drums, tooting their bugles. They were Pioneers heading for the huge parade on the main square.

The column stretched as far as the eye could see. Banners swayed above their heads. The Young Communist members leading the march set the pace and kept the children in neat formation.

The policeman threw his hand up to his helmet to salute. The children fluttered their flags in response, laughing and smiling.

'Hurrah!' they cheered, their cries firing into the sky like a salvo of shots in salute. 'Hurrah! Hurrah!'

'What's wrong?' Shura asked the old woman. 'They can't see us. Come on.'

But the old woman looked at the children as they laughed. Her lips turned pale, even blue.

'Children,' she said.

The children walked by, waving. They stamped their feet as they marched. They jostled with one another and turned their heads to look proudly at the traffic stopping to watch them pass.

'What?' asked Shura, confused.

'I've realized what it is. They need children.'

Everything started spinning before Shura's eyes. As this

idea sank into Shura's mind, he felt more and more dizzy. The crossroads started drifting around, spinning like a huge carousel.

But the students kept on coming, beating their drums, tooting their horns, their cries ripping the air apart.

'Hurrah! Hurrah! Hurrah!'

A portrait floated above their heads: the same moustache and beaky nose. Beneath the portrait in bold letters were the words: STALIN – FRIEND OF THE CHILDREN.

Shura grasped a lamp-post to steady himself.

Friend of the children? The Raven was the children's friend.

The Raven's children! So that's why they took their parents! To steal their children.

They accused their honest mothers and fathers, aunts and uncles, grandmothers and grandfathers of being enemies, saboteurs, spies.

They took their children away and fed them some mysterious slime, gave them new names, dressed them in identical clothes. They muttered the same words to them over and over, until their heads were filled with the same thoughts spinning round like an old record.

Shura realized that the Grey House was nothing but a factory where children were forced into the same, identical mould. They brought in normal children like Tanya, Shura, Bobka, Zoya, Anya, Mitya, and they churned out strange beings that all looked alike with bizarre names like Novembrina, Tractorina and Vladilen. The Raven's children!

It wasn't good, honest, intelligent people that the Raven

needed. He needed humble servants. Children who had forgotten their family and their past. Children who believed that the Raven was their father. That the Raven was the wisest leader in the whole world. That the grey and frightening kingdom of the Raven was the best country in the world.

And Bollard. That nasty, cruel woman. She can't have been living a happy life there – maybe she had lost her family, too. She secretly gazed at a photograph of a lady in a hat and maybe she didn't even remember who it was. Perhaps she had also forgotten her family and everything about her previous existence. She, too, was a daughter of the Raven.

And that's where Bobka was right now. In the Grey House. Where Shura had been. But Shura hadn't seen Bobka there, so the Raven must have had many houses like that. Houses for toddlers like Bobka. For elementary schoolers, like Shura. For many, many other children.

'Bobka,' whispered Shura. And then he shouted: 'Bobka-a-a-a-ah!'

Shura suddenly felt a blow to his stomach as though someone had punched him. It felt like something was erupting inside him and he gagged as it rushed up to his throat. Shura bent over, his mouth stretched open as though he were about to be sick. But, instead of vomit, out of his mouth slithered a strange grey creature, which plopped to the ground, like a writhing sausage. Shura was shocked to see it wriggle away, this strange fat worm with a mouth gaping wide, full of tiny sharp teeth.

'*Aaaaaaaaaaagh!*' groaned Shura with horror.

He felt his stomach lurch again. He belched and out flopped a second little grey sausage-shaped worm.

'Mama!' the old woman cried, alarmed at the sight, and fainted.

Shura hunched up, writhing with cramps. He clutched his stomach as he retched and yet another worm flopped out on to the ground. And now a whole stream of them was pouring out of Shura's mouth, wriggling away in every direction.

I'm going to die! Shura trembled with disgust.

And yet, once he'd got these horrible creatures out, Shura felt better, somehow lighter; he had rid himself of the thoughts that had been lurking deep within him. Shura watched, stunned, as the worms slithered away – the lies and fears that had been gnawing away inside him, inside everyone, for so long, fed to him by the Raven's people. They had fed him these sinister thoughts dressed up with noble phrases like 'our homeland', 'patriotic heroes', 'the people'. It was only once they'd settled deep inside you that they grew and grew, and started to suck away at your soul.

Maybe it was these worms gnawing away inside people that made them start to see enemies everywhere they looked, made them suspect their neighbours were spies, even their own parents. Why else, when people were taken away in the night, would their neighbours rush to assume that they were guilty? Nobody doubted that what the Raven was doing was right and proper. No one argued, no one spoke out. They were too afraid. Everyone believed with all their hearts in the Raven – with a passion and with fear.

Or maybe there was no Raven? Maybe he didn't even exist? Not as a bird, or as a human. Maybe there was no beak, no wings – just human hands. Maybe all this was the work of ordinary people. They allowed these horrid things to happen because they didn't speak out to stop it. People didn't dare to help their neighbours, they rushed to turn away and ignore them when they were in need . . . and that hung over the people like a poisonous cloud, a permanently dull grey sky.

Shura's knees trembled. Inside he had nothing left but pain. And yet somehow he felt better. Yes, he was sure of it.

Shura slowly straightened up. He stood a moment, not letting go of the lamp-post. He wiped his mouth with his sleeve.

The Pioneers kept on marching past. They kept on beating their drums, their laughter flowing. The cheerful policeman still held his hand up to his helmet in salute. The grey sky was still frowning. Grey houses looked on blindly.

At last the end of the column was in sight. The Pioneer leader bringing up the rear stomped past in her forage cap, waving a flag in each hand.

'Hurrah! Hurrah! Hurrah!' Their cheers rose up to the sky.

What grey faces they have, these little raven chicks, Shura noticed.

The policeman waved his baton. The cars and pedestrians stirred back into motion. The square came back to life, like a numb leg waking up again.

Shura crouched down beside the old woman. Her eyes were closed. Her chest was rising and falling ever so slightly. Shura breathed a sigh of relief: she was alive!

'Wake up, wake up!' He shook her gently. How embarrassing to have given her such a fright.

The old woman opened her eyes. She raised herself up on her elbows.

'Oh, goodness me. I'm covered in dirt . . .'

She began to brush herself down. She leant on Shura's arm as she stood up. She straightened her hat. Flustered, she started to explain. 'My head started spinning.' She blushed. 'I'm not as young as I once was. And I tend to forget it.'

She seemed to think she had imagined everything. Shura understood how she felt.

'I feel better now,' the old woman assured him. 'Let's go. We'll take the tram. It goes straight over Trinity Bridge, to the fortress itself.'

Shura shook his head.

'Why? What's wrong?'

He didn't answer.

'Don't worry,' the old woman encouraged him. 'It won't take more than an hour.' And, again without receiving an answer, she began to console him. 'Don't worry. Your aunt will be delighted to see you.'

The old woman didn't want to rush him. But she didn't understand.

'You can't stay here with us,' she said cautiously. 'We're already old. You have your whole life ahead of you. You can't be invisible forever. You need to be with everyone else. Go to a regular school and become somebody. Live life together with everyone else. There's little joy to be had when no one can see you.'

Shura faltered. She was right.

'Let's go.' The old woman held out her slender gloved hand. 'Well?'

Shura slowly raised his arm, and almost took the old woman's hand. She smiled. She looked at him with sympathy.

'I understand everything. Don't be sad. Your brother . . . he's still too small to understand. He will have already forgotten you all.'

Shura stepped away from her, jolting suddenly as though a snowball had hit him on the neck. He knew he had to go. He started to run.

'Boy! Stop! Where are you going?'

But Shura wasn't listening.

'Come back! Don't be crazy!'

Ignoring the old woman's cries, Shura ran across the road. The King didn't know how to find the Grey House. But Shura did.

CHAPTER TEN

The sky swelled with grey storm clouds. Rain was on its way. After getting lost briefly in the grid of straight, greyish backstreets, Shura happened upon the broad avenue he was hoping to find. He came to the side street he wanted and the familiar building. The home of the only person in Leningrad he could talk to.

Lena opened the door immediately. The joy on her face faded like a flower.

'Oh, it's you . . .' she muttered. She looked at the stairwell and listened out. Then she quickly whispered, 'Come in, then – don't just stand there.'

Nothing had changed in her room. The same curtains. The bed behind the screen. The table in the centre of the room with a heavy fringed tablecloth.

Lena poured Shura some tea. She spread butter on a bread roll. Her eyes darted about nervously.

She's acting strange today, Shura thought. But he was in a hurry to tell her his plan for saving Bobka.

Shura chattered away telling her what he had realized and how he needed to get Bobka out of the Grey House – pausing only to take another bite of bread, which he barely chewed before washing it down with tea. Lena hovered by the table, pacing from one side to the other.

'That's great. Now come on. Eat up quickly,' she said in a fraught whisper. 'Oh my . . . How slowly you chew!'

Shura stopped. The rain tapped on the windowsill.

Lena shuddered. 'Ugh!' She pressed her fingers on her temples. 'Listen, I'm not trying to get rid of you,' she said softly. 'But . . .'

Shura could tell from her tone that something bad had happened. Lena's voice was full of fear.

She glanced anxiously over her shoulder at the wall.

'You just can't be here,' she whispered. 'We can't be seen together.'

She couldn't bear it any longer. With a clatter, she unfolded the screen to cover the wall. That must be where the eyes usually appeared.

'You and I,' said Lena, pointing to Shura then herself, back and forth. 'We're both on our own. You understand? They took my husband and they took your parents,' she added, still pointing as she spoke. 'But one plus one makes two. And that makes an *organization*. And there are special punishments for any kind of organization.'

Shura put down his cup.

'Don't look at me like that! I can't help you! I can't! Don't you see? I need to be here. So he'll find me in the same place after ten years. Otherwise, we'll never meet again! Do you understand?'

Shura felt sorry for her. She wasn't afraid for herself.

'I understand,' he said softly. 'I'll go.'

She yanked the chair away from the table and sat down.

She sighed. 'Finish eating first.'

It was only then that Shura noticed the jacket on the back of her chair. Looking closer, he saw it was a military uniform with blue badges on the shoulders and stripes on the collar.

Shura felt the bread in his mouth turn to clay. Lena had become one of them! Lena, who was waiting so patiently. Lena! Whose beloved they had stolen away.

Or maybe it wasn't her uniform? Maybe she'd just been asked to wash it, clean it, iron it . . .?

Uh-oh, it's all over. This is the end. His heart thumped in his chest. Lena caught his eye. She turned to see what he was looking at.

'Ah,' she said bitterly. 'You've seen it. Great.' She looked away. 'Don't worry,' she said with a strained smile. 'I won't report you.'

She looked at the window. Raindrops were streaming down the glass.

Shura was relieved, but his thoughts were more with her. *Had she been forced to work for them?* It wasn't enough for them that Lena had to wait ten years. That she shuddered at every knock on the door. That she ran to the phone every time it rang. They had also made her work for them.

Shura realized something painful: you're vulnerable when you're in love. When you're in love, people can trample all over you.

He slid off his chair and stood up.

'Finish eating,' Lena repeated. She sat there at the table, hunched over.

Shura walked over and hugged her. Tears ran from his eyes. And Lena, buried in his shoulder, sobbed loudly. As though Shura were the grown-up. As though there were someone who could help her.

They stood up and both cried together and the rain was crying outside. Shura didn't let go until Lena had stopped sobbing.

'Let me at least get you some food to take with you.' Lena blew her nose. She wiped her reddened face with the palm of her hand.

'No, don't worry,' answered Shura. 'I'll manage.'

'Don't fib.' Lena didn't know what he had learnt from the King about fending for himself.

She went to the sideboard. She cut some slices of bread and spread them with butter and jam. Shura watched her in silence. Lena laid the slices together to make sandwiches. She found a sheet of brown paper and wrapped them up. It seemed to her the least she could do. She began to tie the bundle up with string. Her hands moved slowly. After tying the knot, she began to smooth down the ends of the string. It was as if she was deliberately delaying, as if she couldn't decide what to do.

'All right,' Lena said finally. Her arms dropped to her sides as she thought for a moment. She took a deep breath, then turned to Shura. 'There's one thing I can do for you.' Lowering her voice to the faintest whisper, she added, 'I'll find the address. But you must never come here again. I'll get it to you.'

She walked over to the chair. She put on her uniform and

began to do up the buttons. Without another word, she walked out, leaving the package of sandwiches on the table.

And so, with Lena's secret help, Shura found out which house Bobka had been taken to. In the daytime, he observed the street. There were little windows in the basement along the length of the building. The bigger windows were half-painted with grey paint; you couldn't see from the street what was happening inside, and from inside you couldn't see out.

Shura waited, not really knowing what he was waiting for. After a while, a cat jumped gently to the ground from the top of a basement window. Presumably there were rats in this Grey House, too. The cat, of course, was also grey. It lifted its tail and strutted away haughtily – as though it were well aware that its services were required.

If the cat could go in and out of the Grey House, that meant there must have been a window left unlocked. *I'm in luck*, thought Shura.

He waited until it was dark. With the palm of his hand he pressed carefully against each of the basement windows to see if any budged. One gave way.

Shura carefully squeezed in through the small opening. He dangled there a moment, clinging on to the window frame.

The night watched him through the glass. All Shura could see outside was a patch of tarmac.

Shura stretched his toes down, checking for a firm surface to land on. He couldn't feel anything. It could be just a short drop down to the floor. Or perhaps it was several metres.

He let go.

Something hit his knees. Shura landed in a squat and froze. His fall had sent a ripple through the darkness and the silence. He listened. Not a peep. Nothing stirred. The Grey House was sound asleep.

Shura took off his boots and pushed them against the wall. Around him, in the small room, he could see heaps of crates, sacks and boxes. A patch of moonlight shone on a pile of cans. He was in the pantry. Obviously not everyone in the Grey House ate the same grey slime and grey bread.

Shura dragged a few crates over to the window. He checked that he could climb up high enough to get out again.

Carefully opening the door, he peered out into the corridor. The walls were clear. No eyes, no ears.

Next, he took off his scarf and tied it to the handle of the door, so he would be able to find it again. Then he began to tiptoe along the corridor.

Shura wasn't worried about the scarf being found in the morning. He had no intention of staying there until then.

He crept silently along the dark corridor and up the stairs, regularly checking the walls as he went. In one place, it seemed to him that the surface of the wall swelled as two closed eyelids emerged. Shura stopped. He waited. The wall smoothed out. He carried on.

Far ahead there was a table lamp with a green shade. He heard snoring.

That meant that just a bit further on were the children's dorms. It was fortunate that the Raven loved having everything the same. This house was no different from the

Grey House. In fact, it could easily have been Bollard sitting there snoring at the table with the lamp.

Shura hesitated. He steadied himself against the wall. He froze. Two buds emerged from the wall opposite and began to unfurl.

He held his breath. Two ears fidgeted from side to side. They twisted and stretched towards the snoring. They listened for a moment. But, distracted by the snoring and not picking up anything suspicious, they curled up and withdrew back into the wall.

On tiptoes, Shura stole past the sleeping warden in the corridor. Up close her snore was deafening.

He quietly opened the door a fraction and slipped in through the slim gap. He froze, pausing a moment to let his eyes get used to the even darker dark.

Inside the dorm were endless rows of identical beds. The same grey, square blankets. The same shaved heads. The Raven wanted these heads to be filled with identical dreams.

Is Bobka here? Is one of these sleeping children my little brother?

It was now that Shura suddenly felt afraid. What if he didn't recognize Bobka? If he picked up the wrong little boy by mistake? Or a little girl? It was hard enough in normal circumstances to tell whether a toddler was a boy or a girl, but without any hair and in identical pyjamas, not to mention in the dark . . . And what if the child screamed?

His heart pounding, Shura walked cautiously between the beds. He leant over each one, peering at the sleeping faces. He felt the little ones' warm sleepy breath on his cheeks.

Bobka! Here he is!

Shura was ecstatic with relief, amazed that he had found him so quickly. He took a moment just to look at him. Bobka slept as though he were concentrating on something serious. His faint, blond eyebrows were even knitted into a frown.

Shura carefully peeled back the blanket. And almost screamed. Two round eyes burst open and stared at him.

'Who are you?' Bobka asked.

'Shhh,' whispered Shura, startled. *It can't be!* Bobka didn't recognize him.

'Who are you?' his little brother repeated. Bobka's lower lip trembled.

Shura knew well what would come next. *Now he's going to kick off*, he thought in horror. The wardens would come running, the guards . . .

'No one,' Shura said. 'This is just a dream.'

Bobka's lip stopped trembling.

'You're not real?'

'No.'

Bobka looked at him in amazement. He had probably never had a dream like this before.

'Get up. But very quietly,' whispered Shura.

'I can't,' Bobka said seriously. 'I'll get a smack.'

'You can. You're asleep,' Shura reassured him. 'In a dream, everything is possible. Sometimes you can even fly.'

Bobka nodded. He lowered his legs to the floor.

'Come with me.' Shura took his hand.

Bobka's hand used to be chubby, like a little cushion, but now Shura could feel his bones. It was like holding a sparrow. Sorrow pierced Shura's heart.

'Very quietly,' he reminded his little brother.

'Why?' Bobka was surprised. 'It's my dream.'

This was annoyingly familiar. Bobka always irritated everyone with his exasperating questions. But the thought that this was Bobka, with his stupid questions, made Shura very happy.

'This is the kind of dream where you have to walk very quietly,' the older brother explained. 'It's a game, you see?'

This time Bobka got it.

They crept between the beds. To the door left ajar.

'Where are we going?' asked Bobka, not finished with his questions.

'You'll see! It's very nice.'

They slipped out of the bedroom. Bobka's bare feet slapped on the floor.

They passed the snoring warden. She gave an especially loud snort. Then fell silent.

Shura froze. He heard a loud knocking, a heavy beating sound, and waited, petrified, for the ears or eyes to appear, for the alarm to sound – and that would be the end. But there was no other sound. *It's my heart beating!* Shura suddenly realized.

Bobka stuck his finger in his nose. He looked bored. He was tired of standing still. He looked like he was about to whimper – Shura just had time to press his palm over his mouth.

The snoring rumbled on again. Shura took a deep breath. He tugged Bobka along by hand.

The cone of light cast by the table lamp was now behind them. They quickly slipped round the corner into the corridor. Everything was dark, dark, dark. Even the moon didn't shine in through the windows that stretched high up to the ceiling.

Which way now? Left? Or was it right? Shura panicked. He couldn't remember which way he had come!

He chose at random, dragging his brother behind him. Bobka could barely keep up, with his little legs.

In the dark corridor, Bobka began to whine. 'Where are we going? I'm cold! I don't want this dream any more.'

Shura stopped. Something flashed up ahead. It looked like two small, bright lights.

'*Mia-o-o-o-ow!*' came a low howl.

Bobka whimpered.

'It's OK, Bobka. It's just a cat!'

The cat sprang towards them on silent paws.

'Alarm!' she screeched.

'Shut it, you vile beast!' Shura hissed.

The cat arched her back. '*Mia-o-o-o-ow!* They're escaping! Warden!' she wailed. An ear-piercing '*Mia-o-o-o-ow!*' flew along the corridor, echoing off the hard surfaces.

Shura and Bobka pressed themselves against the wall. Suddenly, from floor to ceiling, the wall was filled with bright, twinkling eyes. They blinked, peering into the darkness.

'This is a horrible dream. I don't want it any more!' moaned Bobka.

Great, that's all I need!

Now the giant ears had emerged and were flapping about like burdock leaves.

A great din started up somewhere further along the corridor. Doors slamming.

'*Mia-o-o-o-ow! Mia-o-o-o-ow!*' screeched the cat like a siren. She kept her green eyes fixed on Shura and Bobka. Her whiskers twitched over her pointed fangs.

There was the heavy thud of footsteps. Then more. It sounded like a lot of feet.

The huge warden appeared out of the darkness. The grey colour of her overalls looked lighter in the dark.

'There they are!' she bellowed. 'Seize them!'

Shura threw himself desperately at the cat. He grabbed the creature's soft, strangely flexible body. He swung his arm, the cat in his hand.

Claws lashed out at Shura's cheek. But too late. Shura let go and the cat flew at the warden, like a grey fur bomb, digging her claws in as she landed on her head.

'Aaaaagh!' roared the warden. She stamped and spun round, trying to shake off the cat. Both hands plunged into the soft ball of fur on her head. But the crazed cat dug in her claws, clinging to the warden for dear life, as though she were riding a bicycle that was out of control.

Below, in the darkness, came a very faint sound of laughter, a snigger that sounded like tiny metal ball bearings being scattered on the floor.

The warden rushed along the corridor with the stunned cat on her head, unable to see where she was going and howling in pain. The cat's tail fluttered in her face like a pennant flag.

From somewhere in the darkness came the sound of more feet. More wardens?

'Let's get out of here!' shouted Shura. But Bobka could not move for fright.

Shura picked up his little brother and ran.

He flew along the corridor at full pelt. Bobka must have realized that this was no dream, and fell silent. It was so dark that Shura felt like he was running on the spot. The sound of footsteps echoed around. Menacing eyes glared at them from the walls. Bobka seemed to get heavier and heavier. Shura's arms were starting to feel numb.

I can't do this any more, Shura realized with horror.

Then came the pursuit: a roar of stomping and yelling.

Suddenly, all at once, the ceiling lamps encased in wire mesh burst into life. The corridor was flooded with light.

'There they are!' someone shouted. 'Seize them!'

Shura was dazzled for a moment. He stopped, blinking until he could open his eyes properly. *It's all over,* was his only thought.

'Hey, Fool! Hey! Yes, you! Fool!' squeaked a tiny voice. A rat was tugging at his trouser leg. It must have been the same one that had sniggered at the infamous defeat of the cat. She giggled. 'We rats all know each other. I've heard about you. You must be Fool, right?'

It wasn't clear exactly what her friend from the other Grey House had told her about Shura, but this rat seemed to be convinced that 'Fool' was his name.

Shura didn't have the strength to protest. He looked hopefully at the rodent.

'Oi, Fool! Over here!' The rat swished her tail.

Shura saw a gap in the wall on one side of the corridor. It was a staircase leading down. The basement!

He charged down the steps. His arms ached. But Shura was scared to death of dropping Bobka.

Behind them the rat carefully hopped down from step to step; they were on the large side for her.

Shura nearly collapsed under the weight of Bobka. His feet kept going, stumbling forward. That was the last step. Another corridor, and it was reassuringly dark. But where now? To the right? Or left?

The rat seemed to have fallen behind. Now Shura had no one to help him. He lowered Bobka to the floor and crouched, offering Bobka his back.

'Climb on. Hold tight.'

Bobka obediently threw his arms around his brother's neck and leant on his back.

What if I can't stand up? Shura started to feel terrified. Holding Bobka under his knees, he put his weight forward as he straightened up. Bobka's heavy breathing was loud in his ears. Shura tried to make himself imagine it wasn't Bobka on his back but a rucksack.

He stood for a moment, trying to remember which way the warden had rushed for help upstairs, with the cat clinging to her head. That way spelled trouble. Shura needed to run the opposite way.

Shura shook as he hauled Bobka higher on his back. *He's got heavy!*

Bobka groaned.

'Hold on. Not long now,' said Shura, either to his brother or to himself.

The corridor seemed never-ending. Shura could no longer run, he just plodded forward with heavy feet. His back arched over. Bobka's hot, skinny arms squeezed his neck.

Refusing to give up, Shura dragged himself onward. But he knew that with every step he was moving further away from the door where he had tied his scarf to the door-handle. From the pantry. From the open window to the street.

He just kept going, carrying Bobka on his back. Onward. Into the darkness. Into the unknown. What else could he do?

'Are we going to Mama?' asked Bobka.

'Sort of.' Shura hitched his brother higher up, tightening his grip around his legs. 'It's all right, Bobka. Don't worry. We can always sleep in the tarmac cauldrons. They're cosy and warm. And we can sit out the days in an attic. Or a basement. And I'll get food for you,' he went on. 'You won't believe the tricks I've learnt! We'll live a good life – even better than with the King. We'll live like kings, Bobka.'

His brother listened attentively. His trusting warmth spread over Shura's body.

If we ever get out of here, that is . . .

Shura leant against the wall, panting. His back was soaked with sweat. His hands were shaking. Bobka was slipping down.

The rat, meanwhile, had safely descended the stairs. She scampered along the corridor to catch up and leapt up on to Shura's leg. He flinched as he felt a tickle run up his thigh. The rat deftly climbed from his trousers on to his sleeve and up on to his shoulder.

'Calm down,' said the rat. 'No need to squirm!'

Bobka had never seen a rat so close up. He stared at her with wide eyes.

'Go on, then!' the rat ordered Shura, directly into his ear, which was like the mouth of a huge trumpet next to her. She looked extremely pleased with herself, perching so high up.

'Where to?' said Shura, squinting at her.

'Straight on!'

Shura clenched his teeth and carried on going.

The rat picked up some kind of muffled sound. It was still far enough away that Shura's human ears hadn't sensed it. It was more like a vibration in the air that tickled the rat's whisker-antennae. She pricked up her ears. She knew that noise.

'Quickly!'

'I'm running as fast as I can,' Shura muttered. His legs were barely obeying him.

Shura gathered his determination into clenched fists. *Left, right. Left, right*, he commanded his feet. Sweat dripped in his eyes. Bobka's hot breath was making his neck clammy. His little hands were suffocating him.

Is there no end to this corridor?

Suddenly it seemed to Shura that he could see some kind of light in the darkness. Perhaps not even light. Perhaps just that the darkness there wasn't so dense.

'Faster,' the rat whistled in his ear.

Shura could hear the noise now. They were being followed! But children's voices? He was amazed. It was children shouting.

'Catch the spies!'

'Hurrah!'

The wardens had set the children on them!

There was a buzzing sound and the ceiling lamps burst into life, illuminating the entire length of the corridor with its rough stone walls. Angry eyes glared at them from the walls. Clear, menacing, merciless eyes. They'd been spotted.

Bobka shivered.

'Run!' squealed the rat.

Shaking with fatigue, Shura's legs staggered along, step by step. He stumbled and fell flat on the stone floor. Pain shot through his grazed knees and elbows. The rat flew from his shoulder over his head. Bobka's weight crushed Shura, though the fall hadn't hurt him.

Shura somehow pulled himself out from underneath Bobka. He stood up. His palms were grazed. His knees and elbows were smarting.

He grasped his brother's hand. He took a moment to catch his breath.

'Bobka, don't look! Don't look!'

The children were behind them, chasing them. Hordes of them, in grey pyjamas, with shaved heads. But most terrifying of all was that they had completely identical faces. As if stamped by a mould. And they were faces distorted by malice.

Shura ran, dragging Bobka along behind him.

'Hurra-a-a-ah!' The roar hit them in the back like a hail of stones.

Suddenly Shura dug his heels in to stop. Miraculously he managed to slow down and hold Bobka back, too.

The corridor came to an abrupt end, and the floor completely fell away into a bottomless abyss. The sky above was what Shura had taken for a light at the end of the corridor.

Bobka started to hiccup in fear.

On the other side of the precipice, Shura could see green trees. He saw houses: pastel pinks and yellows, with white columns, Leningrad-style. The world over there was filled with colour again. And the sky – full of seagulls like folded handkerchiefs – although it was grey, seemed a completely different sky to the one over the Raven's city. The not-Leningrad. The not-Leningrad sky was like murky clouded glass. Whereas this sky was grey-blue, fresh and clear.

Should we jump?

The houses and trees were like toy models; they were so tiny in the distance.

The Raven's children were approaching like a rumbling, grey wave.

'*Keep going straight ahead. And don't be afraid*' – Shura reminded himself of the other rat's advice. *It worked last time . . . But where now? Straight ahead?*

Shura held Bobka closer to him. The grey wave was approaching. The shrieks swelled to a mighty roar behind him.

'Seagulls! Dear Comrade Seagulls!' Shura begged.

The seagulls hung in the air, unruffled by his pleas, just quivering their wings a little now and then to maintain their position. And yet a gust of wind seemed to drag them closer.

'Seagulls, take us to the other shore!'

No answer.

'Please!'

No answer.

'At least take my brother!'

At these words, Bobka clung even tighter to Shura's leg.

'Alone! Alone! Alone!' the seagulls screeched as they flapped their wings. It wasn't clear from their voices whether they were cackling with laughter or crying.

'Have pity on us!' shouted Shura.

But his words were drowned out by the screams of the Raven's children. They were hot on their heels. Shura could already make out their identical goggling eyes. Their identical mouths baring their teeth.

Bobka trembled against Shura's leg.

One seagull started noisily beating her strong wings, holding her body against the wind. Her round yellow eyes gazed enigmatically at the children.

'This! Way!' she cried with each thrust of her wings. 'Each! Must! Pass! Alone! Alone! Alone!' She spread her wings and let herself drift off on the wind.

'Hurra-a-a-ah!' came the Raven's children's deafening roar. The ones at the back were zealously pushing forward. The first were already reaching out to grab their victims, anticipating the moment when they would close their fingers on them. These loyal followers were almost at their heels, their eyes burning with menacing glee.

Bobka screamed. His fear gave Shura strength. He looked down in desperation.

But what was this? Suddenly a flight of steps shimmered before him in the air. Shura could still see through them to the deep dark abyss below. Was he imagining it? He jumped back. The stairs disappeared. He took a step forward. The stairs flickered back into view.

At that moment several small, determined grey hands grabbed Bobka by the pyjamas. Shura swiped at them. Amid howls, the hands let go for a second.

Seizing Bobka in his arms, Shura rushed forward. He waited for his foot to fall, for Bobka and him to hurtle down into the void.

But his foot landed on firm ground. He felt a solid step beneath his sole. Then another. And another.

The steps appeared as he ran. And melted away as soon as he lifted his foot.

'Don't look, Bobka. Just don't look down.'

A few grey figures were about to lurch after them. They almost tumbled down off the edge. But their comrades grasped their pyjamas and dragged them back. And now the herd of children only shook with anger, shouting something, their toes on the very brink of the abyss. They didn't dare step any further.

Behind him, Shura heard a whistle. A drum. He glanced back to see the grey figures lining up in a straight column and marching back along the corridor. The light went out. All that remained was a black wall.

'Keep going, keep going,' whispered Shura.

The steps beneath his feet formed into a fragile floating bridge without railings.

So, this is what it means to be brave, Shura thought. *When you are very, very afraid, but you still keep going.*

Bobka looked around, up at his brother, at the sky, at the seagulls in flight with their legs stretched back. Shura felt his brother's hand in his – trusting, no longer afraid.

It's good when you're little, Shura thought, marvelling at his little brother's innocence and fearlessness. He himself could barely take another step.

The bridge started to curve downward. The city was no longer visible straight ahead.

When the bridge came to an end, right in front of them was a door. Shura opened it.

It was a corridor. The walls were painted up to the middle with a dreary, dark-green paint. The lamps on the ceiling were covered with a wire-mesh cage.

Shura gulped, loudly. *No, not this. Not again!*

He and Bobka walked forward, their footsteps sounding on the floor tiles, echoing off the walls. Diffused beams of daylight shone through the small windows near the ceiling. They cast little squares of light on to the floor. Banners were draped along the walls proclaiming some message or other.

Another door. It was covered with leatherette, studded with tacks like the buttons on a quilt.

Shura pushed it open. And he froze.

In the high-ceilinged room, full of light, a huge woman in uniform sat at a table beneath a portrait of a large-nosed, moustached man with the inscription: FRIEND OF THE CHILDREN. She was writing something.

The woman looked up at Shura and Bobka, disgruntled.

'Here they are – your . . .' she said sullenly, swallowing the last word, as though it were something distasteful.

Sitting beside the table on a wooden bench were . . . Tanya and Auntie Vera!

Shura and Bobka froze. It couldn't be true. It had to be a trap. A stealthy trap of the vilest kind.

Bobka hid behind Shura.

Tanya cried out, but Auntie Vera glared at her. Tanya sat up straight, pressing her back against the hard bench.

Auntie Vera was wearing a beret and looked rather pale. It made her bright red lipstick stand out against her face.

It seemed like the uniformed woman was very irritated by Auntie Vera's bold red lips.

'You can still change your mind, citizen,' she said.

'Where do I sign?' Auntie Vera answered in a dry, cold voice – the one she usually reserved for tram conductors.

The uniformed woman gave a scornful grunt. She dipped her pen in the inkwell. She handed the pen to Auntie Vera.

The ink coughed and spluttered. Auntie Vera wrote her full name. The woman slammed a large purple stamp down on to it.

'Take away your . . .' she said, not finishing her sentence, as though she couldn't bear to mention them. And she began to tidy up her papers, knocking the pile against the table to level out the sheets. She tucked them away into a file, which she closed with a snap.

Auntie Vera stood up.

'You are taking a risk,' the woman said darkly.

Auntie Vera stared down at her.

'What is the risk? Explain to me right now, like one Soviet citizen to another.' Auntie Vera had light-coloured eyes, rimmed with black, and deep dark pupils. Her stare unsettled everyone, whether it was street dogs, policemen or teachers. 'Well?'

The woman in the grey uniform replied with only a grimace. She waved her hand at Bobka and Shura as if to dismiss them.

'Off you go.'

Auntie Vera took Shura with one hand, and Bobka with the other.

Tanya stood and stared at Shura and Bobka, unable to take her eyes off them.

There were no hugs, no tears. Together they walked out into the street.

ABOUT THE AUTHOR

YULIA YAKOVLEVA used to be a columnist and an editor for leading Russian newspapers and magazines and has been an international writer-in-residence for London's Royal Court Theatre. She writes in both Russian and Norwegian, lives with her family in Norway, and received an MA in Children's Illustration in 2017.

The Raven's Children was inspired by true events from Yulia's family's past. Her great-grandfather was arrested and executed under Stalin's regime; his wife succumbed to illness and then death soon after, having struggled to survive under the extreme stigmatization that followed her husband's sentence.

Consequently, Yulia's grandfather and his three siblings were taken to an orphanage for children born to 'enemies of the state'. He successfully escaped and, Yulia believes, became part of an underground gang (the only evidence of this being a scar on his neck, from where he brutally removed a mysterious tattoo, and his knowledge of the 'thieves' language', a now-archaic criminal lingo in Russia). Yulia's grandfather eventually found his siblings, scattered across different orphanages, and reunited with them before becoming the head of the family.

However, he never spoke about these events directly and refused to answer any questions about this period. There was nothing but silence on the matter and he died leaving so many questions unanswered. It wasn't just Yulia's grandfather's story that was silenced and kept from the family. Her mother's grandfather spent ten years in a labour camp, somewhere close to the polar circle, and only survived due to his expertise in growing tropical plants, which kept him in good favour with the camp's chef who needed fresh vegetables. Again, all of Yulia's questions about her great-grandfather's astonishing story were met with silence and deflections.

Yulia found she was not alone and that many Russian families had lived, and continue to live, under the same kind of silence: a refusal from those who have lived through these traumatic and horrific times to discuss their past. This is why she wrote *The Raven's Children* – to fill these gaps, to create a voice that will break the silence, and hopefully to encourage others to share their own unspoken experiences.

A NOTE FROM THE TRANSLATOR

The Raven's Children is a gripping story about a family in the
Soviet Union in the 1930s, a very dark time in Russian history
when thousands, indeed millions, of innocent people were
arrested for being 'enemies of the state' and sent to the Gulag
labour camps in Siberia. This era is known as Stalin's Great
Terror. Seven-year-old Shura and nine-year-old Tanya wake
up one morning to find their parents and little brother have
disappeared in the night, and they have no idea why. All they
know is what they overhear the neighbours whispering:
their parents were taken by the Black Raven. What can they
do except go and find this mysterious Raven and demand he
hands their parents back?

Historically, 'the Black Raven' was a euphemism for the
black cars driven by the secret police when they arrested
people in the middle of the night. But Shura and Tanya
don't know that, nor do they know why people always
whisper about 'the Raven' as though they are afraid to
mention his name. Yulia Yakovleva superbly captures the
fear and suspicion that pervades a tyrannical police state –
and, as the reality that he once knew crumbles around him,
Shura finds himself in an unnerving other world where the

walls literally have ears and eyes, birds can talk, and the relatives of political prisoners become invisible – and untouchable – as they are rejected from society.

When translating I was conscious that Russian children would at least be able to ask their parents or grandparents about the Black Raven and other details of Soviet life. However, this history would not be so obvious to British readers. So, together with the brilliant editors at Puffin, I found ways to squeeze in subtle hints about the Raven actually being a car, although Shura imagines it as a scary bird-man with a touch of Stalin. We added these hints while still staying true to Shura's point of view and without spoiling the suspense and the mystery.

The city of Leningrad (now St Petersburg) is alive in this book and it's a very tangible setting – it's almost a character in its own right. It's ironic that St Petersburg, which was built by Peter the Great to be a window on to Europe, is full of a sense of being closed off by the Iron Curtain, of being a shut-down police state. But you certainly don't need to know anything about Russia to appreciate the story and to empathize with Shura and Tanya in their scary predicament.

While the story is about Russian history and repression under Stalin, it is universal in how it deals with the psychological effect of living under leaders with unchecked power, in dictatorships where people are deprived of civil rights and of control over their own fate. What is exceptional about this book is how it focuses on a child's (incredibly resilient) response to this trauma.

Ruth Ahmedzai Kemp

DISCUSSION QUESTIONS

Chapter One

He never told Valya about it, even though he was his best friend.
Valya is Shura's best friend. What do you learn about the two boys in this chapter? How are they similar and/or different?

They both felt uneasy. Those were definitely people's eyes. People staring out.
Who do you think is inside the freight train? What significance might this have for the story? Explore the other hints of unease and tension in this chapter.

'Maybe it's a map?' said Shura. 'Buried treasure?'
Shura's papa burns the note that someone throws out of the freight train. What do you think was so important and dangerous about its contents that it needed to be destroyed?

'No ice cream for you this month . . . And I'm afraid there'll be no cinema for you either, for a whole month.'

Do you think that Shura's punishment is fair? From what we have learned about Shura, do you think that Shura will obey his father?

Chapter Two

The day was smiling and it smelt of spring.

Throughout the story, the author uses colourful descriptions and language to bring the city of Leningrad to life. How does the author capture the city's excitement at the coming parade?

'Just look at them,' insisted the man.

Shura finds the stranger 'a funny fellow', whereas Tanya later believes that he was a spy who tried to poison Shura. What is your opinion of the stranger that Shura meets? Do you think he was a good person?

. . . and then there was their street with its good, reassuring Soviet name, Pravda Street – Truth Street.

Shura lives on 'Truth Street'. Do you think that anyone tells Shura the truth in this chapter?

Chapter Three

'Mama! Hurrah!' Shura ran up and threw his arms around her.
Usually Mama works until the evening, but in this chapter she's left work to come home, and has lunch with Shura and Tanya. How does the author create tension in this scene?

'Tanya, what does petit bourgeois *mean?' asked Shura.*
Auntie Rita is labelled 'petit bourgeois'. Why might she have been given this label – and why might the theme of judging people be significant?

'Mama's probably gone to work – that's all.'
The children are confused by the disappearance of their loved ones. What do you think has happened to Papa, Mama and Bobka?

'But, Tanya, the old woman might have got it wrong.'
Shura talks Tanya out of going to Auntie Vera's. Do you think that Shura made the right decision?

Chapter Four

'No one would help me. It was like they couldn't see me or hear me.'
Why might the grown-ups in this chapter, such as the neighbours and the policeman, be acting negatively towards the children? Do you think that such behaviour is justified?

243

'The Black Raven is a raven, and that's a big crow, right? And since crows and ravens are birds, let's go and ask the birds about him!'

How does the scene with the crows challenge our expectations of the storytelling? Does this revelation change our predictions of how the story might develop?

Chapter Five

'Why aren't we allowed in? We are Soviet children!'

The Pioneers represent one possible future for Tanya and Shura. What is your opinion of the Pioneers? And what do you think it means to be a good 'Soviet child'?

There was a narrow white strip of paper on the door, with something carelessly scribbled on it in illegible purple ink.

Barriers and obstructions are a theme of this chapter. How does the author use these to create drama and tension – and further highlight the children's predicament?

'Left alone! Left alone!' the pigeons murmured among themselves. They always seemed to be in agreement.

The different birds in this chapter are given their own personality. How might these personalities match with some of the characters that we have encountered in the story?

Chapter Six

The caretaker didn't look at them. He looked down as he swept the slushy ground with his broom.

What evidence is there in this chapter – and previous chapters – of people putting on an outward show? Why might this have become a way of life in Soviet Leningrad?

'I know,' said Shura, as reluctant as his sister to start heading the right way.

Do you agree with Tanya and Shura's reasons for not travelling to their aunt's?

Because in the Soviet Union everyone was equal.

What does it mean that 'everyone was equal' in the Soviet Union? Is it possible for everyone to live equally? What are the pros and cons of such a way of living?

. . . it was still a game. It was still possible to go back. To win the game.

By the end of this chapter, do you think the children still view their predicament as a game? Was Shura right to hand himself into 'the Raven'?

Chapter Seven

'. . . Here you will be made into a man. You will be re-educated.'
Shura is taken to the 'Grey House' to be re-educated. How is his identity gradually erased throughout this chapter?

It appeared that the Raven loved the colour grey.
Everything in Shura's world becomes grey and dull. What events help to awaken Shura and encourage him to escape? And how do these moments contrast with those of the Grey House?

Shura did everything he could to distract himself from thinking about food. But hunger dug its claws into his stomach.
The harsh life of the workhouse starts to affect Shura. How does the author convey this through the use of fantastical elements? Do you think this is an effective technique?

The photograph and this podgy hand belonged to two different worlds.
Who do you think is pictured in Bollard's photograph? What might this tell us about Bollard's character – and does this change your opinion of her?

Chapter Eight

'It's autumn!' He was amazed. 'How long was I there, at the Grey House?'
How has the feel and character of the city changed, compared to its depiction in earlier chapters?

It didn't hurt; it didn't even tickle. It was as though nothing had happened.
Shura and Lena have become invisible. Why might the author have chosen to depict them in this way? What does it mean for their characters?

Lena's eyes twinkled with joy, as if she wanted to light up Shura's path.
How does the author use Lena and Shura's relationship to further explore the themes of truth and hope?

Chapter Nine

'We had a grand piano,' he said. 'In the dining room. And . . .'
Who is the 'King of the Street'? What do you think his background might be – and is there any significance to his title, 'the King'?

'They don't want to see us, so they don't.'
At what point in the story do you think Shura started to become invisible?

'You want me to make you Prince of the Street?' he asked on another occasion.

In what ways do Shura and the King benefit from their partnership?

The King didn't know how to find the Grey House. But Shura did.
By the end of the chapter, the King and Shura have very different reasons for wanting to go to the Grey House. How does it highlight the differences in their characters at this point?

Chapter Ten

'. . . Sometimes it helps to think something up and play along, in order to hide from what is really the case.'
These are Tanya's words to Shura in Chapter Seven. What instances can you think of throughout the story where characters have pretended that things are different from how they really are? Which of the fantastical events and images that Shura has experienced do you think are real and which might be his imagination? How might reality have been different from how Shura perceived or remembered it? In an alternative version of reality, what might have happened to Shura when he tried to rescue Bobka?

'Hey, Fool! Hey! Yes, you! Fool!' squeaked a tiny voice. *A rat was tugging at his trouser leg.*

The story of *The Raven's Children* mixes the real world with fantasy. This type of storytelling is known as 'magic realism'. Why might the author have chosen to tell her story in this way? Do you like stories with fantastical elements?

There were no hugs, no tears. Together they walked out into the street.

Shura is finally united with Tanya and his auntie. Do you think the story has a happy ending for Shura? How do you picture what his life will be like living with Auntie Vera?

★